"[...] my dad?"

A horde of women had cornered Robert in the men's room, convinced they'd found the errant duke from TV and each determined to drag the world's most eligible bachelor to the altar. Much as Sydney liked seeing him suffer, she couldn't stand to see the anxiety in the girl's eyes. "I promise, sweetie. You stay here."

Sydney swung open the door to the restaurant, assuming an air of curious interest. "Hey," she called to the women, "did the duke have a red cap on?" At their nods she continued, "I saw him running across the parking lot!"

Screaming, they almost trampled her as they ran past.

As soon as she was alone, she broke out in a big grin and leaned casually against the men's room door. "Oh, my lord duke?" she called in the sappiest voice, "come out, come out, wherever you are."

ABOUT THE AUTHOR

When Judy Christenberry created the unlikely characters Peter and Robert Morris—part Wild West cowboy, part English duke brothers—she knew each of them had to have his own story. Peter tangled with their mother, the dowager duchess, in American Romance #726, *A Cowboy at Heart*, and now it's Robert's turn to fend off the matchmaking matron who plastered his picture all over America as the world's most eligible bachelor.

Judy is the mother of two grown daughters. She lives in Texas—which explains why she writes so well about her beloved cowboys.

Books by Judy Christenberry

HARLEQUIN AMERICAN ROMANCE

*4 Brides for 4 Brothers

Don't miss any of our special offers. Write to us at the following address for information on our newest releases.

Harlequin Reader Service
U.S.: 3010 Walden Ave., P.O. Box 1325, Buffalo, NY 14269
Canadian: P.O. Box 609, Fort Erie, Ont. L2A 5X3

My Daddy
the Duke

JUDY CHRISTENBERRY

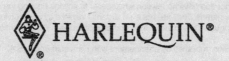

HARLEQUIN®

TORONTO • NEW YORK • LONDON
AMSTERDAM • PARIS • SYDNEY • HAMBURG
STOCKHOLM • ATHENS • TOKYO • MILAN • MADRID
PRAGUE • WARSAW • BUDAPEST • AUCKLAND

To Bill and Peggy Heid,
a gentleman trucker and his wife,
who invited me into their home and the truck
and answered all my questions.
Thanks so much.

ISBN 0-373-16735-0

MY DADDY THE DUKE

Copyright © 1998 by Judy Russell Christenberry.

Printed in U.S.A.

Chapter One

A noise awakened her.

Sydney Thomas frowned in the darkness as she listened intently. Nothing other than the normal night sounds she heard when she slept on the side of the road.

She let her eyelids drift shut and curled more tightly into the warm nest she'd made in the bed behind the driver's seat.

Crunch!

This time she popped up and stared out into the darkness. The noise was repeated. The sound of footsteps on the gravel that lined the road. Had he found her?

Perhaps she'd have been safer at a roadside rest area, but she just couldn't bring herself to join the other drivers these days.

"Breathe deeply," she muttered to herself. After all, the doors were locked and the windows rolled up. In fact, with the motor running to keep the cool air flowing through the cab of her eighteen-wheeler, it was a wonder she'd heard anything.

But she had.

"I'm safe. No one can get in here," she reminded herself. A man would be foolish to try.

Just in case, she reached under the bed for the box she kept there. Pushing off the lid, she pulled out the small pistol that would ensure her safety.

The noise drew closer, and this time it sounded like more than one person. She'd read about gangs preying on unsuspecting travelers. And someone had already announced his intention to harm her. Well, they were in for a shock if anyone thought she'd roll over and play dead.

She pulled on her jeans, all she'd taken off for her rest, and shoved her feet into her battered sneakers. Then she peeked through the curtains she used to shield her bed from anyone looking into the cab of the truck.

There was a glow near her right front fender that had to be coming from a flashlight. But she couldn't see the person holding it because of the size of her rig.

What if they damaged her tires? She should slip behind the wheel and drive away right now. But before she could even move, the cab rocked. Someone was climbing on her rig. She jumped into the passenger's seat, gun at the ready. No one was going to damage her truck.

Staring into a light shone straight on her, Sydney shouted, "Get away from my truck before I blow you away!"

"Don't shoot my dad!" a tiny soprano voice shrieked.

ROBERT MORRIS, the Duke of Hereford, quickly abandoned his climb. So quickly in fact, that he landed on his backside in the gravel.

"Dad, are you all right?" Penelope raced to his side from the hiding place he'd devised behind the trunk of a nearby tree.

"I'm fine, love. Get back behind the tree." He scrambled to his feet, and looked into the window of the lorry above him.

The glass lowered. Instead of the burly truck driver he'd expected, he saw again the vision he'd discovered with his trusty torch.

"What are you doing?" she demanded. Only the slightest tremble in her throaty voice told him she was disturbed by their arrival. That and the pistol she was still pointing in his direction.

"Looking for assistance."

"You're English."

Bloody hell! He'd forgotten to hide his accent. "Uh, yeah," he said, doing his best to sound like the cowboys on his brother's ranch. "But I've been here a long time."

The pistol was still pointed at him.

"Do you mind putting that thing away? It's making me nervous."

The woman stared at him and then the pistol. She didn't do as he asked, but she did lower it so he would only lose a few toes—not a vital organ—if it went off.

"Assistance with what?" The woman ignored his plea. "And where's the child?"

He didn't want Pen coming near the woman. Obviously his idea to seek out assistance in the middle of the night wasn't one of his brightest decisions.

"Um, she's over there," he said, gesturing vaguely into the darkness.

"What are you doing on the road at night with a child?"

"Trying to reach a hotel," he muttered with disgust. What did the woman think? Was she accusing him of some dastardly deed?

"What happened?"

Obviously this woman was not of the school of hospitality before all else. Most Americans were amazingly hospitable to him, he had discovered through the years when he'd visited.

"Look, Miss, I apologize for disturbing you. We'll be on our way." He backed away from the rig, shutting off the torch.

"You've got at least a fifteen-mile walk in that direction," she said clearly, her words filling the night air.

"Surely there must be a house closer than that."

"How were you traveling?"

"By car. It broke down several miles back." He thought about the rental car with identifying tags that had been plastered all over the papers. He wasn't disappointed to be rid of the machine, but he wished it had been less inconvenient.

"How far if we go the other direction?" he asked quickly.

"Probably twenty miles." Her voice was nonchalant. No wonder. She was safe in her automotive castle.

"Bloody hell!" he muttered beneath his breath.

"Ooh, Dad, Nana says you shouldn't—"

"Quiet, Pen," he ordered, his voice stern.

"How old are you?" the beautiful voice asked, floating into the darkness of the night.

Irrepressible Penelope answered at once. "I'm six. How old are you?"

A warm chuckle stirred Robert's senses.

"A lot older than you."

"Come along, Penelope." He began dragging the pile of luggage.

"But, Dad, I'm tired."

"There's no help for it, poppet. Come along."

"Wait," said the woman in the truck.

He halted and stared back at the huge lorry. "Yes?"

"You could—" She hesitated. "You could stay here in my truck. I'll be ready to roll at six a.m. I can drop you off in Toledo where I stop for breakfast."

"Can we, Dad? Can we? I'm very tired," Penelope pleaded, immediately going into her acting mode, her shoulders drooping and an adorable pout on her lips.

Of course, he could be misjudging her. After all, she was only six, and they'd walked several miles. He looked at the woman again. "I would appreciate your generosity. And I promise we won't take advantage of you."

"No, I guessed that."

Her curious words filled him with questions, but he was too busy trying to contain Penelope's eagerness as she surged toward the truck.

"Just a moment, Pen," he cautioned. He tugged the luggage back to the door now invitingly opened to him and his daughter. "Uh, why have you decided to trust us?"

After all, maybe she was the one with evil intentions.

"Because I don't know of any bad guys who bring their kids along or have Louis Vuitton luggage with them when they're up to no good."

He was surprised that she knew the famous label, then was ashamed of his snobbish thought. It reminded him too much of his mother. It was phenomenally expensive, but his mother considered it the only luggage to own.

But he played dumb. "Louis Vuitton—is that good? I bought these at an estate sale." Would she believe such a ridiculous story?

"Lucky you." She nodded toward Penelope, now at his side. "Now why don't you help your daughter up?"

SYDNEY ALMOST LAUGHED as she waited for him to do as she asked. His suspicious stare confirmed her impression. He was concerned about *her* being the bad guy.

Which was reassuring to her. "It's all right," she promised softly. "I won't lock you out once I've got her in my clutches."

She was the one who should be nervous. After all, she was breaking her long-standing rules: always travel alone and never pick up any strangers. But certain circumstances made the idea of company more appealing.

Besides, she couldn't leave a six-year-old stranded on the side of the road in the middle of the night. And how could anyone as handsome as this child's daddy be evil?

No, she knew better than that.

He swung his daughter up in his arms for a hug before he lifted her toward Sydney. She pulled the little girl, doll-like in the moonlight, into the seat with her.

"Do you mind if I bring up the luggage?" her father asked.

"Of course not. Hand it up and I'll stow it away." She told Penelope to get on the bed and turned back to the open door. In minutes the luggage rested on the floor between the two seats.

Before the man could join them, Sydney began shifting several of the cases beneath the bed. He had climbed into the passenger's seat, and she, without thinking, leaned across him to lock the door.

He withdrew like a virgin under attack.

She sat back in the driver's seat, blinking her eyes. Had she imagined his reaction? It wasn't that she wanted him to come on to her—even if he was handsome. But she knew she was considered attractive by most men. Why had he flinched?

"I always keep my doors locked," she explained breathlessly.

"Of course. Wise precaution. Penelope?"

His child stuck her head through the hanging curtains. "I'm here, Dad. She has a little room in here. There's a bed and everything."

Sydney pulled back one side of the curtain and fastened the holder. "That's right. That's where I live when I'm driving." She turned toward the man now sitting across from her in the passenger's seat. "I'm Sydney."

He grew still, as if taken by surprise. Then he responded, "I'm Robert and, as you know, this is Penelope."

Sydney felt a tug on her sleeve.

"There's no bathroom," Penelope whispered, an anguished look on her face.

Sydney understood the difficulty at once. "Ah. No, there's not. We have to use natural facilities at times like these."

"What does she mean, Dad?" the little girl asked, as if Sydney had spoken a foreign language.

Perhaps she had. While the man had denied having come recently from England, his child had a pure, delightful English accent. Surely *she* was lately arrived from the motherland.

"Uh, she means you, uh, take care of business behind a, uh, tree."

"Outside?" Penelope asked, her eyes widening in surprise as her voice rose. "Where everyone can see you?"

"There's no one to watch but your father and I'm sure he'll promise to look the other way. Come on."

"But it's dark!"

"Yes, but you were out in the dark and you didn't get hurt." When her logic appeared to have no affect on the child, she turned to the man. "May we borrow your flashlight? It might ease Penelope's worries."

He quickly handed it over. "I could—"

"No, that's quite all right. Just promise to let us back in in a few minutes." She'd meant her words as a joke, but somehow a new uneasiness filled her. Of course he would let them back in. She had his daughter.

Once they'd reached Penelope's tree and Sydney had explained the basics, she turned off the flashlight and waited. Penelope began to chatter as she emerged from her first experience with an outside bathroom. "Do you use trees like this all the time?"

"Seldom, really. I stop at gas stations."

"Gas stations? Is that where you buy petrol? Why would that—"

"They have public restrooms I can use."

"Oh. Are they lovely?"

"No, not particularly," Sydney returned with a smile. This little lady hadn't experienced much in life.

"Dad's torch is very good, isn't it? I'm not scared when it's on. I can see everything."

"Yes, it's a good—torch. Hurry now. I have to get my sleep so I can drive in the morning." She used the flashlight to check the time. Almost two o'clock.

"Why were you and your dad traveling so late? Did you need to be somewhere tomorrow?"

"No. At least I don't think so. But that lady wouldn't leave us alone."

Penelope didn't show the least concern for "that lady" now, so Sydney didn't attach any significance to her words. They climbed back into the cab of the truck.

"You didn't look, did you, Dad?" Penelope demanded at once.

Sydney almost laughed when the unsuspecting father was roused from sleep. "What?"

"Your dad fell asleep, so I don't think he looked."

"Oh, good." The little girl patted him on the shoulder, a gentle touch that said a lot for their relationship. It reminded Sydney of her relationship with her own father. At Penelope's age, Sydney had thought she was responsible for her father's care.

"You need to rest because you had to carry our luggage. Are you comfortable?"

The man shot Sydney a wry look. "She's training to be a flight attendant," he growled.

"Ooh! I'd like that," Penelope assured him. "But Nana wouldn't approve."

"Not one word about your damned grandmother, Penelope!" he replied, anger filling his voice.

At the harshness of his tone Sydney wondered if she'd been overly generous in her acceptance of these two.

He must have noted her reaction. "I'm sorry," he said. "My mother has put me in a devilish predicament."

"At least you have a mother who can—" She stopped abruptly, not wanting to complete the sentence. She did know where the words—or the sentiment—had come from, but it was a subject she didn't discuss with anyone.

"If you don't mind, I'll give you some pillows and you can sleep in the seat. It won't be the most comfortable, but—"

"It will be preferable to walking a dark road all night long," he finished. "Thank you."

"Penelope can sleep with me. I'll be up in a few hours, and we'll have you back to civilization in no time," she assured him, her voice determinedly cheerful. "Ready, Penny?"

"I get to sleep in the bed?"

"You surely do. You're so little, I figure you won't take up much room."

The child seemed delighted with her plans. Sydney opened the small closet and pulled out a T-shirt for Penelope to use as a nightgown, then helped the child change. Penelope immediately insisted on showing her father.

"Very nice, dear. I hope you thanked our hostess."

"Of course. Nana always says I mustn't forget."

"Your Nana sounds like a very nice lady," Sydney said, smiling at the little girl.

"You're only saying that because you haven't met her," the man muttered.

Sydney gave him a cool stare. These continued remarks about his mother were very ill-mannered.

Once she had Penelope tucked into the bed, she handed a pillow to the other guest. She winced as he shifted in the seat to find a comfortable perch, knowing how his back would feel in the morning.

Then she dropped the curtain and slipped off her sneakers and jeans.

"Aren't you going to put on pajamas?" a little voice whispered.

"No. I don't have long to sleep. I'll try to be quiet when I get up in the morning so I won't disturb you."

In the darkness, she heard the rustling of the sheet, then felt warm rosebud lips on her cheek. "Good night."

Sydney lay silent, reveling in such a mundane yet trusting act. Almost immediately, the sound of deep, even breathing told her Penelope had drifted off.

Sydney cupped her cheek, holding the warmth of the child's touch to her. How long had it been since she'd been touched by such sweetness? How long would it be again?

She didn't want to think about it.

"Uh, Sydney?"

Surely he didn't intend to come on to her now that his daughter was asleep!

"I think you'd better put this away. Penelope is a terribly curious child."

In the darkness she could barely discern his hand coming through the curtain. But the silver gun barrel picked up the pale moonlight coming through the side window.

"Oh! I—I forgot. Thank you."

"Thank you," he said quietly, withdrawing his hand after she'd gripped the gun.

Surely, if nothing else, his return of her weapon proved he had no ill intentions toward her. After storing the gun away, she settled down onto her pillow.

Of the two things offered by the man and his child, she thought the most dangerous might be the kiss Penelope had bestowed upon her.

ROBERT SQUIRMED, wondering what had awakened him this time. His hours in the seat had frequently resembled torture. The pillow behind his back helped, and he used the other to rest his head against the window. But he was still uncomfortable.

He only had his mother to blame for his difficulties. Already, he'd decided he hadn't been nearly sympathetic enough to Pete when *he* was under attack. At the time, Robert had already survived his mother's attention and was trapped in a miserable marriage his mother had brought about.

Now he was determined to outwit her. She wasn't going to marry him off a second time. His brother was producing the necessary heir for the dukedom. There was no longer a need for Robert to remarry.

Besides, times were changing. He believed his own child, Penelope, should be allowed to inherit his estate. Not that he hadn't provided for her—but their home, the title and the farms would go to Pete's son.

In fact, his not having an heir had made him agree to his mother's matchmaking the first time. Besides, Celia had seemed lovely—a beautiful young woman who understood her role as a duchess. And she'd understood a lot more than had Robert.

She'd understood wealth, lovers, betrayal.

His parents had had an unusual marriage, frequently striking sparks. His mother, the daughter of a wealthy rancher from Montana, had refused to put up with royal traditions and had loved her husband to distraction. Robert had hoped his marriage would do as well.

Instead, all he'd gotten were the traditions. No heart.

Now his mother hoped to force him into marriage again. Only this time, since he was coming to America, she'd decided to find him an American bride. A picture of his present hostess flashed into his mind. Not what his mother had in mind, of course, but Sydney was a beauty even in jeans and a T-shirt. She had an elegance in her movements that he found attractive.

He dismissed such thoughts. He certainly shouldn't entertain such sensual ideas about a brief acquaintance. He had to reach his brother's house for the birth of his heir. Then he would return to England and resume his life. His plans were made.

The only question remaining was whether he could escape the trap the dowager duchess had set for him. Tonight, at least, he had. And if he kept off the main roads and avoided all major hotels, managed to rent another car without using his credit cards... Hell, he didn't know what he was going to do.

Just as his eyelids drifted closed in despair, he sensed movement near him. His eyes jerked open as the curtain behind him shifted.

When the woman emerged into the early morning light, he realized his torch hadn't flattered her nearly enough. Her clear soft skin begged to be touched, and her hair, a warm brown with traces of red, was plaited in a long braid down her back. Wisps danced around her head, giving her an ethereal appearance.

Like an angel.

He shifted upright, causing her to jump.

"Sorry, I didn't mean to scare you."

"And I didn't mean to wake you. Feel free to slip into the bed with Penelope, if you want. I'm sure your back is crying for a flat surface." She flashed him a smile that lit up her face, but it disappeared all too soon.

Dismissing the sudden attraction that rose in him, he considered her offer. He was tempted, because she was right about his back. But he felt it would be rude to seek comfort while their rescuer worked. "Not at all. I was most comfortable."

She shot him a grin that good-naturedly accused him of lying. "Suit yourself."

Without another word to him, she set about checking the various dials. Then, with a roar of the motor, she eased the big lorry back onto the highway.

Fascinated with her, he said, "I thought you had to be muscular to drive one of these."

She cocked one russet eyebrow at him, drawing his attention to the blue of her eyes. "I am."

He didn't know whether to laugh or to challenge her. Instead, he chose to remain silent. Did talking disturb her? He didn't know anything about her except that she was kind, which made it difficult to enter into casual conversation. But his gaze kept returning to her soft curves.

Looking around the cab for something other than this beautiful woman to occupy his thoughts, he noticed the newspaper on the floorboard between their seats.

Bloody hell! Everything was going to be ruined now!

Grabbing the paper, he turned it over across his lap. "Do you mind if I read this paper?"

"Of course not. It's yesterday's, but I like to pick them up as I travel." Her gaze never left the road.

Keeping his eye on her, he folded back the top page of the first section, hiding the screaming headlines from her view. "Do you read them each day?"

"Sometimes. I didn't get a chance to read that one."

And he'd make sure she never did.

Chapter Two

Sydney eased into her usual parking space at the truck stop she frequented on the outskirts of Toledo. Once the big rig had come to a halt, she looked over at her handsome passenger.

Halfway to Toledo, he'd drifted back to sleep. The paper he'd been reading had slipped to the floor. Penelope hadn't been heard from at all and presumably was still sleeping, too.

So, breaking her rule hadn't hurt her, Sydney admitted with a sigh. She'd send these two safely on their way, and she wouldn't be worrying about leaving them out on the highway, unprotected.

She ignored the tremor of anxiety that ran through her at the thought of being alone again herself.

She shut down the motor, creating a rare silence. Then she eased herself from the driver's seat, picking up the fallen newspaper on her way, folding it and putting it in the bottom of her closet where she stored papers for recycling.

It was time to wake up her passengers. Deciding to tackle the easiest one first, she slipped behind the

curtain and studied the curled figure of Penelope. A
sweet longing filled Sydney. She loved children. As
a second grade elementary teacher during the school
year, she spent her time with the innocents of the
world. Some were already not as innocent as she'd
like, but they were full of hope and love.

She'd always dreamed of having her own family
one day. Now she didn't think that would be possible.

Before she fell into a depression, she leaned over
and shook Penelope's shoulder. "Penny? Time to
wake up, sweetheart."

The little girl's eyes fluttered open and she stared
blankly at Sydney until recognition dawned. She sat
up and looked around. "I really slept in your truck,
didn't I? Did you drive?"

"Yes, I've been driving for a couple of hours.
We're in Toledo now, where you and your dad can
get a new car."

"What's a Toledo?"

"It's a city in Ohio, one of our states. Come on,
here are your clothes. Get dressed and I'll wake your
dad."

She slipped back through the curtains and gingerly
touched the man on his shoulder. "Um, Robert,
we're in Toledo."

He jumped, his eyes flying open. "Why did you
let me sleep?" he demanded in a rough tone.

"I thought you must be tired. There wasn't anything you could do to help me," she said, staring at
him.

"Oh." He straightened in the seat, then looked at her sharply. "Where's the paper I was reading?"

"I put it in the closet. I keep old papers there until I can recycle them."

"You keep old newspapers?" he asked, a faint look of panic in his eyes.

What was the matter with him? Did he have a phobia about papers? She dismissed such ridiculous thoughts. "We're in Toledo. I usually stop here for breakfast. You can call your rental company from here."

"Oh. Of course." He looked out the window. "It looks crowded."

"Not really. These rigs take up a lot of space, but usually there's only one person per rig. And they serve breakfast fast."

"Good. I'm starving."

She blinked in surprise. "I didn't mean you had to eat here. Once you call your rental company, I'm sure—"

"Do you mind if we eat breakfast with you?"

She wondered if he had no money and was hoping she'd pay for their breakfast. Of course she would. She couldn't stand the thought of the little girl going hungry. But something about the odd couple didn't add up. "No, of course not. I told Penelope to get dressed, so—"

"I'm ready," the little girl intervened, opening the curtain.

"Yes, you are," Sydney returned with a smile. "Except maybe we should brush your hair."

"I want to wear my hair like yours," Penelope said, reaching out to stroke the long braid.

"Pen, we don't have time—"

"It won't take but a minute," Sydney assured him. She was flattered by the child's admiration, and it wouldn't take long to put the long silky black hair into a braid.

When the two females emerged from behind the curtain a second time, the man had slipped a baseball cap on his head. It was pulled low, shadowing his eyes.

"Ready?" he asked, his gaze shifting from his daughter to Sydney.

"Yes, we are. And starving, aren't we, Penelope?"

"Yes. I'm going to eat a great big breakfast," the child announced, holding her arms out wide.

Sydney's heart was touched. Money was tight, of course, but she'd never gone hungry. She'd assumed Penelope was naturally delicate, but maybe her thinness came from lack of regular meals.

Her father didn't look malnourished, however. In fact, his body was quite impressive. Sydney assumed he was at least thirty, but he certainly hadn't let his body go to seed. And it was attracting too much of her attention.

She blushed when he caught her staring and immediately hustled her two passengers out the door. The man climbed down the side of the truck and stretched up his arms to receive his child.

Penelope wasn't interested. "I can do it by myself," she asserted.

A sense of déjà vu swept over Sydney. In the summers, she'd ridden with her father and had always wanted to prove her independence by climbing down herself.

"You probably can, Penny," she said, "but it's nice that your dad is there to help."

As he caught his daughter by the waist, the man shot Sydney a look of approval. She turned her back to him to climb down herself, smiling—but that smile disappeared when his hands spanned her waist and lifted her to the ground.

"I can manage on my own," she asserted, surprise roughening her voice. She wasn't used to a man touching her.

"But you said it was nice for him to help," Penelope reminded her.

She opened her mouth to argue the point but Penny's anxious look and the teasing glint in the man's gaze stopped her. "Never mind. Let's go get breakfast."

The café part of the truck stop was half-full and noisy with conversations. Sydney slipped into a booth without waiting for the busy waitress to seat them.

"Hi, Syd," the woman called as she hurried by. "Coffee?"

"Yes, two, please," she ordered, then stopped to look at her companion. "I assume you want coffee. Should I have ordered tea?"

"No! No, I drink coffee," he said, tugging the cap lower on his forehead. Which was a shame because it covered his hair and shaded his gray eyes. She'd already noted his great hair, dark like Penelope's and well cut.

Even as she watched him, he scooted down against the vinyl booth, which made him appear shorter—not easy for a tall, well-built man like him. Penelope was trying to read the menu, so Sydney turned her attention to the child, but she did think Robert was behaving curiously.

"What'll you have?" Wanda, the waitress, demanded as she slapped two mugs of coffee on the table.

"Two eggs over easy, bacon and toast," said Sydney.

"And your gentleman friend?" Wanda asked, leaning closer to him than was necessary and batting her fake eyelashes.

"The same, please," he said in low tones.

"My, don't you talk nice," Wanda exclaimed. "What about the little one?"

"I want pancakes," Penelope announced. "Lots and lots of them."

"Bring her milk also, please," her father ordered.

"Comin' right up. You picked a classy guy, Syd, and a looker, too." Without waiting for Sydney to respond, she dashed back to the kitchen.

"Sorry," Sydney murmured, her cheeks hot. "Wanda leaps to conclusions."

He shrugged.

Another group of truckers entered and sat in the booth next to them. Sydney greeted them, but then quickly turned her attention back to Penelope.

"Hey, Syd, maybe you should look into this," one of the men called from that group.

"What are you talking about, Carl?" she asked cautiously, barely looking his way.

"Haven't you been readin' the papers? There's a duke driving across America lookin' for a bride."

The man held up the front headlines from the Toledo paper. "Look. He's not bad lookin' but there must be something weird about him. With a title and lots of money, you'd think he'd have better luck than me."

Everyone around the table laughed, and several jeering remarks were made about Carl's inability to get a date.

"You still refusin' to go out with me?" Carl called to Sydney.

"I'm afraid so, Carl. It would be like dating my brother." Carl had been a friend of her father's. She could as easily have said like dating her uncle, but she didn't want to hurt his feelings.

"Heard anything else from your secret lover? I thought I heard him last night, callin' for Sweet Lips," the trucker announced, and everyone around his table watched for her reaction.

"I wouldn't know. I didn't have my ears on last night." On purpose. She kept her gaze on Penelope.

"Well, sh—I mean, darn, Syd, how you gonna know if you're interested if you don't listen?"

"I'm not interested. So if you know who this is, you tell them, Carl, okay? I'm not interested."

As if he'd just noticed the man with her, Carl leaned toward them. "Hey, you already caught you someone? Hey, guy, what've you got that us truckers don't have?"

Sydney looked at her companion, ready to intervene if necessary. The teasing could get pretty rough with this group.

Penelope's father, however, seemed to manage. He gestured to his daughter and said, "She took pity on us because of my child."

"Ah, that explains it. I don't have a kid."

"Hey, maybe he's the duke and Syd's stealing a march on everyone," another of the men shouted. "He talks kind of funny."

"Yeah, right, like a duke would hang out around here," a third man chimed in. "He'll be at all the five-star hotels, not Turnpike 80 Truck Stop. No one will be looking for him here."

Amid general laughter, Wanda brought three plates piled with food and set them down in front of Sydney and her guests.

Conversation wasn't expected in a truck stop when the food arrived. Sydney watched Robert, afraid he'd been offended by the conversation. However, he seemed to be lost in his thoughts.

She helped Penelope apply the syrup to her stack of pancakes and cut them up in small, bite-size pieces. "Don't forget to drink your milk," she urged, then silently warned herself against playing the mother.

It didn't take long to polish off breakfast. Wanda, on one of her many dashes by their table, slid them the bill. Sydney reached out for it, ready to pay and get back on the road, and was surprised when her companion grabbed it first.

"What are you doing?" she asked.

"Paying for your breakfast. It's the least I can do since you rescued us."

She stared at him, trying to read his mind. "I thought maybe you were having money problems."

"Not—" He paused before finishing, "Not exactly."

"I'll be happy to pay for breakfast if it'll help."

He shook his head. "I'll pay this and then make a phone call about the car. Could you take Pen to the loo for me?"

"Of course." She slid from the booth and held out her hand to the child. "Come along, sweetie."

As they passed the next booth, Sydney had to endure several comments about what a good mother she would make. Fortunately, the truckers kept their comments PG-rated because of the child.

"Do you want to be my mummy?" Penelope asked, looking up at Sydney even as she followed.

An image of home life with the sexy Robert flashed through her head, surprising her. "I wouldn't have anything against it, but those men were just teasing. They've known me a long time. Just ignore them."

"Nana wants my dad to get married. They had a big argument about it."

"Where's your mom?" Sydney asked, curiosity getting the better of her.

"She's dead. I don't remember her very much."

"Well, your Nana is probably worried about who will take care of you, but it has to be your dad's decision," Sydney said, hoping her words wouldn't create problems.

When they came out of the restroom, they found Penelope's dad waiting for them.

"All ready?" Sydney asked, putting a cheerful smile on her face. She was going to miss the companionship she'd shared the last few hours. And the comfort of knowing she wasn't alone.

"Um, really, there's a spot of trouble. Could I talk to you privately?"

"You mean without, uh—alone?" she asked, her gaze going to Penelope.

He seemed surprised by her interpretation. "No, I meant could we go back to your truck."

"Sure. You'll need to get your luggage out anyway." She frowned when she didn't read agreement in his expression, but she led the way to the parking lot.

When they reached the truck, Penelope danced from one foot to the other, tugging on Sydney's T-shirt. "Can I try to climb up without help? I know I can do it."

"That's up to your dad," Sydney said, not daring to make decisions for the child.

"Yes, all right, love, but be careful," he agreed, distraction in his voice.

"What's wrong?" Sydney asked, taking a step away from Penelope's ascent.

"They don't have a car available this morning."

"Well, there are other car companies. They'll be listed in the Yellow Pages." She turned to follow Penelope, who, by now, had reached the passenger's seat. But Robert held her back with a warm hand on her shoulder.

"Where are you going?" he asked.

"Up there," she said, wondering why he had to ask.

"No, I mean, where are you driving to?"

"Fargo, North Dakota. Then I'm heading to Colorado to pick up a load there." It wasn't her normal run, but she owed Roy, the scheduler, a lot of favors and he'd asked her to take the extra job.

"Ah. We're heading west also. Could we ride with you for a couple of days? It would really help a lot, and I promise we won't be a bother."

Sydney stared at him. She'd thought earlier that there were several things that didn't add up about the man and his child. Lack of money would explain some of them, but then he'd paid for breakfast. Now he wanted to ride in her truck?

"I—that's—I don't know. I never take riders."

"Will it get you in trouble?"

"No, it's my rig. I can do what I want, but—I don't stop much. I have a deadline to meet. Once we reach Fargo, I won't have to press too hard, but I have to be in Colorado in five days.''

"We won't ask you to stop. Penelope is a very good traveler,'' he assured her, an earnest, pleading look in his gray eyes that made it impossible to say no.

Though she tried to marshal arguments against their coming with her, she couldn't voice the most important one. She was used to being on her own, but already she found herself enjoying the company. When they left, she knew she would feel the loneliness even more.

On the other hand, right at this moment, having someone with her might be to her advantage. Especially if she let the crowd inside know that she wasn't alone.

"I suppose it'll be all right,'' she finally agreed with a sigh.

"Thank you, I promise you won't suffer for it, Sydney.'' He paused, but something in her gaze must've made him add, "I apologize if I'm being too informal but I don't know your last name.''

"My name is Sydney Thomas. And I don't know your last name, either.''

It struck her as odd that he stopped, as if she'd asked a complicated question. Then he said, "I told you our names are Robert and Penelope.''

"And your last name?''

He stared across the parking lot, then turned to grin at her. "Lockwood. Robert Lockwood.''

He reached for the holds to pull himself up to the rig. "I'd better tell Pen the good news."

Sydney looked behind her, where Robert had stared before he came up with a name, and noted the Lockwood Trucking Company sign on the rig parked near hers. The man was lying through his hat.

But why?

With a sigh, admitting she'd probably made a mistake, she followed him up into the rig. "I'm going back inside and buy some sandwiches and drinks for lunch. Any particular kind you like?"

"Won't they spoil before we eat again?" he asked.

"We're going to ride with you some more!" Penelope shouted, interrupting their conversation.

"I know. I hope you don't get bored."

"No, I won't. I'll learn how to drive, too. Wait until I tell Nana."

"I doubt that your grandmother will want you to become a truck driver, Penny." She turned to Robert and answered his question. "I have a cooler to keep lunch in. What kind of sandwich do you want?"

"We both like roast beef," Robert said, even as he reached into his wallet. Before Sydney could protest, he pulled out a fifty-dollar bill.

"What are you doing? You paid for breakfast, so I'll buy lunch." She wasn't going to freeload.

"You're providing us with transportation. I'll take care of the food," he said firmly and pressed the money into her hand. "Will that be enough?"

She raised her eyebrows. This man said he'd been

in America a while and he wondered if fifty dollars would be enough to buy sandwiches at a truck stop? "Oh, yes, I think so."

He didn't seem to notice her sarcasm, so she slipped out of the truck and hurried back into the café. The first thing she did was to casually mention to the other truckers that her passengers were staying with her. Her fellow drivers warned against such consideration, but she ignored them.

After buying lunch, she picked up a box of her favorite cookies for dessert. With more than half of Robert's money still unspent, Sydney decided to purchase several things to keep Penelope entertained: some children's books and coloring supplies.

I can think of a few things to keep Robert entertained. Now where did that thought come from? she asked herself.

With a grin, she picked up the Toledo paper Carl had held up earlier. Maybe Robert would enjoy the story about the duke who— She held the paper closer to her.

No! It couldn't be. As one of the truckers had said, who would look for a duke in a truck stop?

But then, she hadn't found him in a truck stop. She had found him along a deserted road in the middle of the night, with his child, toting four Louis Vuitton suitcases.

And now she'd found him again, staring up at her from the front page of the Toledo paper.

Chapter Three

Sydney scanned the article, her gaze frequently returning to the clean-cut, distinguished profile in the picture. His mother had given the interview—which probably explained his anger toward her.

He was a widower, with a six-year-old. Nothing else was mentioned about Penelope. At least his mother had been wise for his child's sake in making no mention of her name.

However, the Dowager Duchess of Hereford hadn't left out much else. She'd detailed his three estates in England; a sugarcane plantation in the Caribbean; his homes in England, France and on the plantation; his wealth—more than Sydney could even contemplate; the factories he owned; and the jewelry his future duchess would have.

Half the women in America must be drooling at the thought.

Whew! Penelope's Nana must really be anxious to marry off her son. But Sydney felt she'd indulged in overkill. With that much bait, the woman probably expected the perfect duchess, but what she'd receive would be hoards of money-hungry females.

When Sydney reached the paragraph describing the hysterical reaction some women had had when they saw the duke, she knew she'd found the reason he wanted to ride in her truck.

No one would look for him there.

Including the press. It seems reporters were pursuing him as much as were the women. They'd published the license plate number of his rental car, and named the hotels he'd stayed at over the last few days and restaurants where he'd dined. The information had been culled from credit card receipts.

Robert couldn't make a move without journalists tracing him.

Unless he rode in her truck.

He could've been honest with her, though, she thought in disgust. Unless he was afraid *she'd* try to marry him. It hurt a little to think he suspected her, too, of searching for a titled husband.

But then, he didn't know her very well.

She stepped up to the checkout counter with the newspaper and her other purchases and asked for a bag of ice. Though there was still money remaining, she didn't buy anything else.

But Robert *Lockwood* was going to get his money's worth when she threw the paper in his lap!

Sydney's righteous indignation that he might suspect her of chasing him lasted about halfway across the parking lot. That's about the time she saw Penelope sitting in her dad's lap, hugging his neck. Instantly, she was assailed by memories of her own father and the closeness they'd shared on their road travels. She hated to upset the little girl.

She slowed down her pace to think. What did it hurt? So he traveled under a disguise. It wasn't going to affect her. Was it? It wasn't as if she had any intention of trapping him into marriage.

She'd even enjoy the company.

Without them you'll be alone again, a little voice warned.

And that other nauseating, insistent voice—the one she feared—would taunt her on the radio, maybe even follow her to wherever she parked that night. What she suspected had probably started out as a joke among a few truckers had turned nasty for one man.

That had been her worry last night. That that man had found her.

She made an abrupt decision, even as she berated herself for her cowardice. She couldn't help it. If she could avoid the nastiness that seemed to follow her these first few weeks on the road, maybe whoever it was would give up his pursuit. Maybe she'd be left alone to earn the money to pay for her mother's care. Maybe she'd be able to keep her promise made to her father as he lay dying.

Could she be convincing? She'd have to make very sure she showed no interest at all in the duke. Which would be difficult since his good looks, and the way he so tenderly cared for his child, already disturbed her peace.

Just think of him as any man, bumming a ride, she warned herself. Yeah, any man with a darling child, sex appeal, and more money than she could ever earn in a lifetime.

"Ready to go?" Robert called to her as she reached the truck.

"Yeah, time to move," she snapped.

His eyebrows rose at her short tone, but he opened his door to lean down for the bag of groceries. "Hand the sack up and I'll store it away."

She did as he asked without saying anything, then remembered she'd put the newspaper in the bag. Hurrying around the truck, she swung up into her seat and said, "Here, I'll get the cooler. By the way, I grabbed a paper for you. I thought I might read it later, after you've finished with it."

As she reached for the cooler under the bed, she watched as he hurriedly lifted the paper from the sack and folded it so the headlines didn't show.

"Thanks. Maybe I'll do the crossword later."

She was glad to have gotten past her impulse to reveal what she knew, but it also irritated her that Robert showed no emotion over his deception. "I bought a couple of things for Penny to do also. Hope you don't mind. Here's your change."

Digging into her pocket, she pulled out the extra money.

"Keep it for future meals."

"No." She left no compromise in her tone. Putting the money in his hands, she then ripped open the bag of ice and poured it in the cooler with lunch. Then she strapped herself in and warned him to do the same. Before he could even move, she was revving up the motor, checking her gauges. Time to be on the road.

"Are you upset about letting us accompany you?" he asked, his gaze steady on her.

"No. But I'm running behind schedule." With that, she flicked on the radio and pulled out of the truck stop.

ROBERT GOT THE MESSAGE loud and clear.

Leave her alone.

She might as well have spoken aloud, he thought. She'd bought things to keep them busy and silent. And she'd been even more standoffish than last night when they first met.

At least she wasn't chasing him, bent on seducing him, like the rest of the women in America. That woman at the hotel yesterday had knocked on the door of his room and pushed her way inside before he'd even grasped her intent. Then she'd started disrobing, making what he supposed she thought were seductive moans.

Pen asked if the woman was sick, which had surprised the hell out of the temptress.

That's when he and Pen had hit the road. After all, that had been his plan all along. He just hadn't realized he'd have to travel *incognito*.

He'd thought their trip to America would be a wonderful opportunity to show Penelope his mother's homeland. And a chance for the two of them to be alone. In England, they were always surrounded by staff, and his days seemed to be one long interruption after another.

Penelope was growing up all too fast. He wanted to keep her close, to share his life with her. And here they were—hiding in a truck, avoiding women.

Once he'd realized the effect his mother's interview was having, he'd considered going straight to the airport and flying to the ranch. His mother had, thankfully, left his exact destination out of the article. But he figured if he bought tickets to Helena, Montana, the press—and the women—would find out.

And follow him straight to Pete's ranch.

He was under no illusion that reporters would respect No Trespassing signs. And while his brother and the cowboys on the ranch could protect him, they wouldn't enjoy the job.

No, better to find another, secret, way to the ranch. Like in a huge lorry. Could he persuade Sydney to take him to the ranch?

He eyed her under his lashes as she drove. That elegant grace he'd earlier noticed made it difficult to believe she was strong enough to control the huge vehicle. And that grace combined with her strength was incredibly sexy. There was also a tense determination in her lips as she pressed them tightly together. If she didn't relax soon, she'd be sore tonight.

"Everything all right?"

"Yes, of course," she snapped, as if angry that he'd intruded.

"Sorry," he apologized.

"No, I'm sorry. I shouldn't take out my troubles on you."

"What troubles?" he asked out of curiosity.

"Nothing. I'm just a grouch in the mornings." She offered him a brief smile and turned her concentration back to the highway taking them out of Toledo, heading west.

"What were those other drivers asking about?"

"What?"

"The item about the secret lover. Have you had a spat with your man?"

"You have a man? Where?" Penelope asked, scooting to the edge of the bed where she'd curled up with the book Sydney had bought her. She even looked under the bed, as if she suspected Sydney had a man hidden there.

Both Sydney and Robert began an answer to satisfy the child, then stopped.

"No, sweetie," Sydney answered finally, "I don't have a man. My friends were teasing me."

Robert waited, but she said nothing else. "Then who were they talking about?"

"Don't you want a boyfriend?" Penelope asked, clearly more intrigued by the conversation than by her book. "Nana says—"

"No, Penelope, we do not want to hear your grandmother's views. She's just a bit balmy."

Sydney swung a big-eyed gaze on him. "You shouldn't say such things about your mother!"

"Even if it's true?" he asked, wry amusement

dancing in his eyes. Obviously she hadn't dealt with his mother.

"You need to be grateful that she's still—that you have family around you."

That gave him pause. Yes, he was grateful he had his mother and Pete. Well, at least Pete. Growing up in England, they'd had an ideal childhood together, and now he missed his brother a great deal. "I do love my mother, Sydney, but she—she interferes in my life."

"That shows she cares about you."

"I could deal with a little less caring." It suddenly struck him that she hadn't mentioned any family herself. "What about *your* mother? Or brothers and sisters. Do you have family who create tumult in your life?"

"No."

He waited again. Nothing. "No one?"

"No."

Unerringly hearing the loneliness in that single word, Penelope slid from the bed and walked the three steps it took to reach Sydney. "We'll be your family, Sydney," she said.

Robert scooped her into his lap. "Don't bother Sydney when she's driving, Pen. That could be dangerous." But he watched Sydney as she blinked furiously, as if trying to hold back tears.

"Thank you, Penny," she finally said softly. "That was very generous of you."

"Nana says—"

"Pen!" Robert warned.

With a sigh, his child subsided against him.

"She'll need to be in the seat belt if she's going to stay with you in the seat," Sydney said briskly, as if she found returning to her driving to be a blessed relief.

Robert sent Penelope back to the bed, suggesting she draw him a picture of Sydney's truck. Fascinated with the idea, Penelope was soon bent over the tablet Sydney had bought, the tip of her tongue at the corner of her mouth as she concentrated.

For several hours, the three of them traveled, each in their own little world. Penelope occasionally showed her father her latest drawing.

Around noon, Sydney suggested father and daughter have a picnic lunch on the bed.

"I even have a plastic tablecloth in the closet behind my seat to protect from spills."

"Can't you have a picnic with us?" Penelope asked, her gaze going longingly to Sydney.

"No, sweetie, I'm not going to stop for lunch. I need to have my truck there before five tomorrow, so I can get it unloaded on time."

"What happens if you get there late?" Robert asked.

"Then I pay for the unloading or do it myself." She sounded matter-of-fact, as if she'd done so in the past.

"Why don't I drive the lor—truck and you picnic with Penelope? She would enjoy it and you could relax for a while."

She turned to stare at him as if he'd suggested overthrowing the government. "What?"

"I suggested—"

"Never mind. I heard you. But I couldn't trust the truck to an inexperienced driver. I have insurance, but it's not that good."

"I've driven big trucks before, Sydney." His quiet assurance didn't go very far.

"Somehow you don't have the appearance of a truck driver," she said. "Are you trained?"

"I'm not licensed, but I drive them on the farm."

"You don't look like a farmer, either. Any other jobs you're qualified for? Maybe lion tamer? Or magician?"

Her sarcasm angered him. He snapped back without thinking. "How about woman tamer?"

Her cheeks paled and she stared straight ahead. Her reaction alarmed him. He hadn't meant anything dastardly. "Sydney, I apologize. I didn't intend— I was irritated."

"Forget it. Just fix lunch for Penelope."

"See here, Sydney. You need to relax. You won't make it if you stay so tense all day. Let me drive for an hour. It's straight road, isn't it? I'll admit I'm not too good on tight maneuvers, but I can manage road like this," he said, gesturing out the window.

She shoved a wisp of hair from her face and let out a big sigh. "Are you sure you can manage?"

"I'm sure."

She continued driving, saying nothing, and Robert thought she'd decided against his suggestion. Then she began downshifting and pulled to a halt beside the road.

Turning, she stared at him. "I'm going to trust you because—because you're right. I've been pushing myself. But if I lose the rig...." She broke off to swallow.

"I won't do anything dangerous," he promised solemnly, realizing how much she was trusting him and unable to dismiss the pride her trust brought him. He was used to people relying on him, but Sydney's trust made him feel elated.

She started out of her seat and he moved at the same time, their two bodies meeting in the middle. Robert reached out to steady her and found his hand brushing against a soft breast.

They both jumped back and Robert almost stumbled over his seat.

Penelope chuckled. "You almost fell, Dad."

"Right," he agreed and plastered himself against the back of his seat, waiting for Sydney to move through—and for his breathing to return to normal. "Uh, go ahead, Sydney. Sorry I got in your way."

She slipped past without looking at him, and he moved into the driver's seat.

He'd expected endless directions, but she stood silently, watching him, and he realized she was waiting for him to show her he hadn't lied.

After checking all the mirrors, he slid the truck into first and moved into the slow lane, picking up speed, changing gears effortlessly.

"You really have driven before," she said, letting out the breath she was holding.

"I don't lie," he assured her sternly and then regretted his words. He could feel his cheeks flushing with guilt.

Fortunately, she ignored him and turned her attention to Penelope.

The two ladies had an enjoyable lunch on the bed. Robert listened to his daughter's chatter and Sydney's gradually more relaxed tones. Then Penelope slipped to his side. "Dad, Sydney's gone to sleep."

Robert glanced in his rearview mirror and saw that sweet, curvaceous form stretched out on the bed. Quickly he drew his gaze away, feeling he was prying. "Can you clean up the lunch mess, Pen? Make sure nothing spills."

"Sure, Dad. Don't you want some lunch?"

"Yes. Can you feed me?"

"Like the monkeys at the zoo?" she asked with a giggle.

"Exactly."

For several hours, much to Penelope's delight, father and daughter played trucker. When that began to bore her, she asked, "Dad, where's that thing that the truckers talk on? Remember, it was on the telly back home."

"Oh. The CB." He scanned the panel of the truck with all its dials and gauges. Finally, down below, he found a knob for the radio the truckers used to communicate. They listened for several minutes to the chatter of various drivers. Then Robert frowned as he realized all the conversation might not be appropriate for his sharp-eared daughter.

"Hey, Sweet Lips," said a voice from the CB, "You got your ears on? I'm followin' you, sexy baby, and tonight you'll find out how I'm gonna tame you, 'cause I'm gonna give it to you hard—"

A slim hand reached between the father and daughter and snapped off the radio. "We don't use the CB," Sydney ordered succinctly.

SYDNEY COULDN'T LOOK either of her passengers in the eye. She was shocked that she'd slept for so long. And she was even more shocked by the words they'd all heard.

"I'll take over now. You shouldn't have let me sleep." In fact, she was amazed that she'd drifted off, as if she actually trusted Robert with her precious truck.

He made no argument, downshifting to bring the truck to a halt. Then he saw the sign up ahead. "There's a roadside park not far from here. Want to stop there for the bathroom facilities?"

"No!"

In his rearview mirror he frowned at her, but she ignored him. She had her reasons. And she was in charge. Just because she'd let him drive didn't mean—

"But I need to go," Penelope protested.

"In just a little while, sweetie, I promise." There was a truck stop ahead—one that was usually safely

crowded. She'd fuel up there and let everyone use
the facilities. Then she would get off the main roads.

"Dad, what did that man mean? Why—"

Both Robert and Sydney hurried to stop Penelope
again. They broke off and Sydney waited for Robert
to take over. After all, Penelope was his child.

"That man wasn't saying nice things, Pen. We
don't want to repeat them or Nana will get very angry."

"But you said we didn't care what Nana thought,"
Penelope recited with a preciseness that almost put a
smile on Sydney's face. Robert was going to pay for
bad-mouthing his mother.

"Not— I mean— I didn't intend for you to think
everything about Nana was wrong!" he protested,
exasperation lacing his voice. He continued easing
the rig to a stop.

When he rose from the driver's seat, Sydney hung
back, staying near the bed until he'd cleared the area.
She didn't want any more collisions like the last
time.

"Have you eaten?" she suddenly asked as she prepared to pull back onto the highway.

"Yes."

"I fed him like a monkey at the zoo," Penelope
said, and continued to tell Sydney about her father's
behavior, giggling about his attempts to emulate the
animals.

It appeared that the little girl had forgotten about
the words on the CB—but Sydney couldn't.

The other truckers were polite, but often teasing,

when she was around them, as she had been most of her life, accompanying her father on trips in the summers. But with the anonymity of the CB, some of them had gone too far. This summer a group of men, all calling her Sweet Lips, had begun to make suggestive calls to her.

And one—the one she'd heard a few minutes ago—had deteriorated from suggestive to threatening.

Which was why she didn't want to stop at the roadside park where the other truckers would be. She wasn't comfortable being around them anymore.

"Sydney?"

She looked at Robert, then glanced back at Penelope who was once again playing with her tablet and colors.

"Yes?"

"I think we need to talk."

He was keeping his voice low so as not to attract his daughter's curiosity, and Sydney instinctively did the same.

"About what?"

"About what's going on. Who that was on the CB? Has that happened before?"

She drew a deep breath. "I think you need to mind your own business." She hadn't meant to sound so abrupt, but if her words kept him from questioning her, she wouldn't regret them.

They didn't.

"I'm not risking my child's safety just because

you don't want to reveal your secrets," he said sternly.

He might as well have punched her in the gut. She was trying to do the two a good deed. But she hadn't even considered that she might be putting Penelope at risk.

Her jaw squared. "The truck stop coming up is near Chicago. I suggest you get out, then, and rent a car."

"Sydney—"

"No. It's for the best."

Nothing more was said, though tension seemed to thicken with each passing moment. Robert stared out his window, and Sydney kept her gaze glued to the road ahead, counting the moments until she would be alone again.

Penelope, who hadn't heard their discussion, sat on the bed drawing and singing to herself in her childish soprano, unaware that everything was about to change.

When she saw the sign up ahead, Sydney braced herself for the parting. Already she was going to miss Penelope. The child was delightful company. And the man beside her had become more than a temporary protector—he'd been thoughtful and kind.

He'd even stirred in her a desire for intimacy she'd thought long gone. Not that that was a good thing. After all, her life didn't provide for relationships.

As she eased off the road into the large parking lot of the truck stop, she noticed another rig closely following her. She shook her head to erase suspicious thoughts. Just because one voice had said he was right behind her didn't mean this trucker was the one. Did it?

She slid a sideways glance toward Robert and realized he was studying the truck behind them, too, out of the side mirror. She hoped he'd forgotten the words on the CB as easily as Penelope had.

After stopping her rig and turning off the engine, she opened her door and slid down to the cement without saying anything to Robert. She rounded the truck and reached up for Penelope as Robert handed the child down.

"Syd! Hey, you behind schedule?" a man's voice called.

She spun around, Penelope in her arms, and faced Carl.

"You're usually ahead of me by a couple of hours and I've been right behind you most of the way," he continued as he climbed down from his rig.

Right behind her? Was it Carl who'd been harassing her?

She heard, rather than saw, Robert climb down. Without a word, he stepped in front of her and faced Carl.

"Was that you on the CB? Because no one should speak to Sydney that way." His jaw was so tightly clenched, Sydney could scarcely detect his English accent.

"What's it to you?" Carl returned, his head thrusting forward like a rooster ready to fight.

Sydney wanted to walk away and pretend she

didn't know either of them, but she couldn't. Robert was a big man, but Carl was like a three-hundred-pound wrestler. She couldn't abandon Robert to face him alone, even though Robert had started the confrontation.

Touching his arm, she tried to silently call Robert off.

Instead of ignoring her, or shaking off her hand, Robert surprised her by wrapping his arm around her shoulders. "It's my business because Sydney is my fiancée."

She thought she was going to faint.

Chapter Four

Robert felt sure he'd gone bonkers. His desire to protect Sydney had prompted his hasty words—a mistake he recognized too late. Good thing Sydney didn't know who he was, or he'd be in real trouble.

But given the chance, he'd do the same thing again. The voice on the CB had been ugly, and Sydney was obviously frightened. How could he protect her if the truckers thought he was merely bumming a ride?

And he wanted to protect her. For all her strength and determination, it appeared she was alone in the world. And yet she'd reached out to him and Pen, not hesitating to help.

"Robert, you—"

"Have the right to protect you," he assured her tightly, unwilling to back down. A real man took care of the women in his life—for however short a time.

"Is that true, Syd? You done gone and agreed to marry this guy? He's a foreigner!" Carl protested. "In fact, I do believe he's that duke feller," he said, leaning closer.

Robert tightened his hold on Sydney. "Don't be absurd. Why would I be riding in a truck if I were a duke?"

"Well, you sure look like him."

Sydney laughed, and Robert hoped that only he heard the tremor under her chuckle. "Everyone has a twin in the world, Carl. Even you."

"Too bad he *ain't* the duke," Carl said, ignoring Sydney's words. "He could help you with your prob—"

"We've got to go," Sydney said, cutting him off. "See you down the road."

She tugged Robert and Penelope after her until they were out of Carl's hearing range.

When they came to a halt, Penelope was the first to speak. "You're going to be my new mummy? And come to England with us?"

The excitement in the child's voice told Robert that his daughter wouldn't object to their phantom plans. But would she be upset to learn the plans weren't real?

Sydney shook her head. "No, sweetie. Your dad was just joking."

"Sydney, I was trying to protect you. That man sounded dangerous."

Sydney turned a cold blue gaze on him, but her hands on her trim hips drew his attention to her curves instead of her words. "I appreciate the sentiment, Robert, but it was a boneheaded gesture."

He stiffened at her comment. He hadn't wanted

her to take him up on marriage, of course, but he didn't think she should insult him.

A shout interrupted his reply. Carl was coming after them, his face animated.

"Hey, Syd! I just thought of something," Carl shouted as he drew nearer. "You're gonna be sellin' your rig, aren't you?"

"What?" she asked, a deep frown on her face.

"You'll be sellin' your rig since you're marryin' this feller, won't you? How much you gonna be askin'?"

The sudden switch in Carl left both Robert and Sydney with their mouths open. They stared at the other man while he studied her rig as if it already had a For Sale sign in its window.

"No—no, I don't think so," Sydney protested.

Robert squeezed her shoulders. "Sydney hasn't decided yet about the truck."

"But when she gets married—"

"Our plans aren't finalized," Robert insisted. "Sydney will give you first refusal when she's ready."

Sydney pushed away from Robert. "I don't need *either* of you conducting my business," she insisted, her full lips pressed together.

Robert wasn't pleased with her reaction. He'd only been trying to assist her. But then he'd already recognized Sydney's independence; he shouldn't have been surprised.

Carl ignored Sydney's response and returned to

the subject that apparently interested him the most. "Yeah, but will you?"

"What? Give you first refusal? Fine. And keep my plans quiet. I don't want everyone knowing just yet."

"Sure, sure," Carl said before turning back to Robert. "And what did you say your name was?"

His gaze fixed on Sydney, Robert blanked out when he tried to come up with the same name he'd given Sydney earlier.

Before his silence became too obvious, Sydney answered for him. "Lockwood. Robert Lockwood."

"Well, congratulations, Lockwood. You've got yourself one fine gal."

To Robert's surprise, Carl extended his hand. Carl now seemed a regular old chap, acting as if he were happy about Sydney's marriage.

Robert shook his hand and then watched as Carl hurried into the truck stop.

A slap on his arm reminded him of the woman beside him.

"I can't believe you let him believe we're engaged," she said, her cheeks flushed and her eyes flashing.

"I didn't hear *you* explaining, either." He halted abruptly when his gaze collided with his daughter's worried frown. With a slight nod in Penelope's direction, Robert changed his answer. "Believe it or not, Sydney, I only wanted to protect you."

"Was that the man who wanted to hurt Sydney?" Penelope asked before Sydney could answer.

"We don't know, sweetie. Your father thought so, and he—"

"Made up the story about marrying Sydney," Robert finished. "I'm sorry, Penelope."

"Robert, we have to tell Carl the truth," Sydney said quietly.

"It's probably too late. Carl has marched into that place with the intent of spreading the news about you as soon as possible."

"I asked him to keep it quiet!"

"And you and I both know that's not going to happen. Do you want to go in and explain?"

"No, of course not," she replied, a frown on her brow.

"We need to get back on the road so you can keep to your schedule." He turned to the truck.

"I thought you were going to rent a car?"

"Not unless you insist."

She stared at him, then nodded. As he walked toward the truck, she asked, "Aren't you coming inside?"

"Yes, as soon as I get my cap. I forgot it when I saw Carl coming over." He certainly didn't want to leave his disguise off now—not when he'd virtually promised to marry Sydney. She might decide to hold him to his promise.

Might? Bloody hell, the women he'd met in America so far would haul him into court so fast his head would spin!

WHEN ROBERT CAME DOWN from the truck the second time, he once again had the baseball cap pulled low over his eyes.

Penelope giggled. "You look funny, Dad. Can you see?"

"Of course I can, Pen. Quite well enough to keep an eye on you. Let's hurry now so we won't hold up Sydney."

Sydney appreciated his concern for her schedule, but confusion reigned in her head. Had Carl revealed anything to his cohorts in the truck stop? She'd soon know. Taking Penelope's hand, she hurried across the parking lot.

The stares she received as soon as the three of them entered told the story. Carl's innocent pose wouldn't have passed muster with a doting parent, much less with Sydney. She glared at him and hustled Penelope to the ladies' room.

Penelope carefully washed her hands, as her nanny had taught her, but her attention was focused on Sydney. "Why don't you have a little girl, Sydney? You'd be a good mummy."

Sydney had been drying her hands, a frown on her face. Now she turned to stare at Penelope. "Thank you, sweetie, but you should be married to have children, you know."

"Can't you find anyone to marry?"

Penelope feared she'd said something wrong, because Sydney's cheeks turned red. Nana had said she should never embarrass anyone.

"I guess not," Sydney finally said.

"Maybe you should marry Dad, like he said. Then

I could have you for my mummy, and Nana would be happy.'' Penelope thought her idea was brilliant.

"I can assure you, Penny, that your Nana would be very unhappy if I married your father.''

"Why?''

"Because I'm not—'' Sydney stopped and pressed her lips together. Then she continued, ''I'm not the kind of bride your grandmother wants for Robert.''

"How do you know? Do you know my Nana?''

"No. It doesn't matter anyway, sweetie. Your dad was being gallant, that's all. He didn't mean it.''

Penelope looked up at Sydney and put her whole heart into her next words. ''I wish he had.''

Sydney hugged her, but said nothing. Taking her by the hand, she led Penelope back to the café. But Penelope vowed to find a way to have Sydney for her mummy. She liked her hugs, her warm smiles, her caring attention.

And she thought her dad liked Sydney, too.

ROBERT WAS WAITING for them when they came out of the restroom.

They bought a few items and hurried out to the truck. In Sydney's opinion, their stop had been a disaster. She wanted to avoid all truckers for a while.

"Dad.'' Penelope said as soon as they were back on the road. She waited until her father turned to her. Sydney watched her in the mirror, filled with uneasiness.

"Yes, Pen?''

"Nana always says you're a gentleman because you're—" She stopped abruptly, her eyes enlarging.

Sydney almost smiled, but she turned away, hoping Robert wouldn't notice anything. She was pretty sure Penelope almost gave away Robert's secret.

"What is it you're trying to say, Pen?" Robert asked quickly.

"I think you should marry Sydney," the child said.

Sydney caught her breath, then turned it into a cough.

Robert said nothing, and she couldn't resist stealing a look at him. That was a mistake, since he was staring at her.

"Why do you think that, Pen?"

His voice was even, calm. Maybe the females of his family plotted against him all the time.

"Because she'd be the best mum. And maybe I could have a brother or sister. And Nana would be happy."

"Those are all good reasons, Pen, but people don't get married for those reasons. Marriage is something for adults to consider, not children."

"You could protect Sydney, too. I don't want anyone to hurt her."

Sydney was touched. She reached out a hand behind her, and Penelope clutched it, coming to stand beside her.

"Sweetie, no one is going to hurt me. I'll protect myself. But I appreciate your wanting me to be safe. It makes me feel good."

"If you're not going to stay on the bed, you'd better come sit in my lap, poppet, and get in the seat belt," Robert said gently.

"Don't you want to protect Sydney?" Penelope asked as she obeyed her father.

Sydney shot Robert another quick glance. Penelope was putting him on the spot. Before she could think of a way to divert the conversation, Robert spoke.

"Yes, poppet, I want to protect Sydney, but I think she can take care of herself."

"But can't you marry Sydney anyway? She would be the very best mummy, Dad. And I would quite like a mummy."

He hugged his daughter close and grinned at Sydney over his child's shoulder. "You and Nana. But that's not a good enough reason to marry, my pet, like Sydney said. So we'll just ignore Dad's crazy behavior, okay?"

With a reluctant nod, Penelope slid from his lap to return to the bed. On her way, she said to Sydney, "If you change your mind, me and Dad would be extra nice to you."

Sydney couldn't resist a hug, too. "I know. You would be a very special daughter, but it's not possible. I'm a truck driver and you and your dad are from England. I can't be driving across that ocean, you know."

Penelope joined her in a chuckle.

CALM SETTLED OVER the cab of the truck as Sydney steered it down the highway. The peacefulness their unlikely trio shared was amazing.

"How late will you drive tonight?" Robert asked.

The peace disintegrated. Somehow, he disturbed her just by talking to her. "We should eat around seven. Then, I'll probably drive until midnight." She shot him a sideways glance before adding, "I don't intend to park at a truck stop tonight, either."

"Wouldn't it be safer surrounded by other drivers?" He kept his voice low to avoid drawing Penelope's attention.

Sydney had debated that question frequently. And although she thought Robert was right, she couldn't bring herself to be around the men she'd counted her friends as she grew up.

She hadn't realized how much she'd depended on the drivers to be her family after her father's death. Perhaps that explained the devastation she felt by being betrayed by one of them.

Which explained why she avoided *all* of them. She didn't know who the enemy was.

"It might be. But I prefer to stay alone." With a shrug, she added, "If you want to stay at a hotel, I can drop you off."

Holding her breath, she waited for his reply. And silently warned herself that she couldn't get too attached to Penelope. Or Robert. Or to having someone with her.

But she already had.

"Tired of us already?" he asked, his voice light, a grin on his sexy lips.

"No, but the accommodations aren't what you're used to, are they?" She didn't really know much about his life except what she'd read in the paper, but it was enough to tell her he didn't usually spend the night in a truck on the side of the road.

"They were quite satisfactory compared to the open road last night."

"Where do you live in England?" She knew she shouldn't press him for details of his life, but it passed the time, giving him the opportunity to come up with lies.

"I have a—" he began, then stopped abruptly. "Pen and I have a house in the country."

"You're really a farmer?" Somehow she couldn't see him all grubby and sweaty. Even after sleeping in the truck last night, he had an air of sophistication about him.

"I have several jobs, but I occasionally put in hours on the farm. That's where I learned to drive big trucks."

His words eased the tension in her. Silly, but it made her laugh inside that he described his life that way. As if he were a working stiff. "I guess we do have something in common." She was teasing him again, but he had no way of knowing that.

"And what is that?"

"Working more than one job. It's hard to make ends meet, isn't it?" She took her gaze off the road to smile at him, enjoying his sudden discomfort.

"Well, uh, that is…"

"Did I offend you? I'm sorry, I was just—"

"What's your other job?" he asked abruptly.

"I teach elementary school during the winter."

"Ah. That explains your care of Penelope. She's quite entranced with you, you know."

"The feeling is mutual," she assured him, glancing into her rearview mirror to see the child working industriously on her drawing.

With a frown, he said, "I understood truckers in the United States did quite well. Why is it necessary for you to also teach school?"

That was a question she didn't want to answer. She kept her financial needs to herself. "I have a lot of bills," she mumbled, staring at the road.

Her attention was fortunate. A small car ahead darted around her, then slammed on the brakes when there wasn't as much space as the driver had thought between him and the car in front of Sydney. Sydney jammed on her brakes, sparks flying. The protesting screech of the machine filled the air as it tried to obey her orders.

"Hold on!" she shouted, worried about her passengers even as she braked. "Penelope!"

Fortunately, Sydney had left a lot of space between her truck and the one in front, but the new car had lessened it considerably. She wrestled with the wheel as she stood on the brakes, but the pressure eased as the first car sped up, giving the little car and Sydney more room.

Sydney continued to apply the brakes, then eased her truck to the side of the road, finally coming to a complete halt and shifting the rig into neutral. "Is Penelope okay?"

"I fell off the bed," the child informed her, an accusing look on her face.

"It wasn't her fault, Pen," Robert assured his child. "She did quite an excellent job of avoiding an accident."

Hearing his praise helped steady Sydney's shakiness. She leaned back and took a deep breath. "I'm sorry, Penny. Did you skin your knee or anything?"

"I'm not bleeding, but my leg hurts," the little girl moaned.

"I don't think she's badly hurt," Robert said, as he released his seat belt and turned to his daughter. "I'm sure it's the suddenness of it all that's upset her." He looked at Sydney with steady gray eyes. "Are you all right?"

Sydney tried to dismiss the sweet sensation of having someone care about her feelings. Since her father died and her fiancé deserted her, there had been no one. "I'm fine. I just need a minute to catch my breath."

"Did you get that driver's license plate number? He should be reported for careless driving."

Sydney smiled. "It's a good thought, but I didn't get it. Even if I had, the public tends to see us truck drivers as the bad guys because we're so big."

Robert straightened, frowning. "But I'm a witness. That would make a difference."

Sydney could laugh at the irony. A witness on the lam. "Thanks for the thought, but no one would pay attention to a hitchhiker. You'd have to be someone important before it would matter.''

Robert frowned, but Pen leaned forward. "But Dad is—"

"Sydney's right, poppet. There's probably nothing to be done."

"But I hurt my leg," Penelope reminded them.

Sydney released her seat belt. "How about a Bugs Bunny Band-Aid? Would that make your leg feel better?"

Penelope cheered up. "Bugs Bunny? Really? I think I hurt my finger, too."

"Then I think we need two Band-Aids, don't you, Robert?"

Gravely, he studied his little girl. "Definitely."

Sydney slipped from her seat and took her first-aid kit from the shelf. She applied the Band-Aids, giving Penelope a third to keep handy just in case she needed it.

Leaving Penelope on the bed, studying her Band-Aids, she climbed back into the driver's seat and started the truck again. She still felt a little shaky, but she had a schedule to keep to.

"Why do you carry Bugs Bunny Band-Aids with you? Do you have a particular fetish I should know about?" Robert asked.

She grinned, letting his teasing lighten the moment. "No, but most kids like them. When I cleaned out my shelves at the end of the school year, I found almost a complete box and put it in my first-aid kit so I wouldn't have to buy new ones."

"Ah. Well, they certainly are a hit with Penelope."

"I'm sorry she got hurt. I guess you probably want to find another way to travel now." Until she said the words, she hadn't realized how much she'd miss the pair.

Robert gave her a sharp look, then turned to study the passing countryside. "Not unless you've decided you don't want company any longer. Did we distract you?"

"No. It was the car's fault."

A comfortable silence fell between them, and Sydney was contemplating spending the next few days with Robert and Penelope—knowing they would leave her eventually, but not yet.

But she'd have to stem her growing attraction to Robert. Even if he were a normal man, he'd be out of her reach. But a duke was so far above as to be ridiculous.

Penny slid to the front of the bed.

"Are you still feeling okay, Penny?" she asked.

"I'm okay. But I think I like traveling in an airplane better, after all. Can we fly to Uncle Peter's ranch, Dad?"

"Of course we can, Pen. If you want to leave Sydney behind." Robert's deep masculine tones assured his child, but did nothing to lift Sydney's spirits.

"Well, that settles it, then, Daddy." Penelope brightened. "You'll have to buy her a ticket, too!"

Chapter Five

"But why can't you come with us?" Penelope asked, childish petulance filling her voice.

"Because it's my job to deliver the load in my truck," Sydney said. It was sweet of the child to want her along, but Sydney had responsibilities. She bit her bottom lip and tried to concentrate on her driving. Even though she didn't look at him, she could feel Robert's gaze on her, and her cheeks heated up.

"But Dad could—"

"No, Pen, I can't do anything about Sydney's job. She made a promise."

"But, Dad, everyone has to do what you say. You're a—"

"Dad who's about to rebuke his only child," he said quickly.

Sydney could hear the panic in his voice. How silly! He still believed she'd trap him into marriage if she knew his true identity. He probably thought she couldn't find anyone to marry her unless she tricked him into it. Hah! Carl had asked her to marry him every summer the last few years when she was driving with her dad.

A brief comparison of the man beside her to Carl made her realize that saying Carl was attracted to her might not impress Robert.

She said nothing.

SYDNEY MEANT NOTHING TO HIM. It was merely his gentlemanly training that insisted he offer his services to her for as long as possible, he told himself.

But honesty forced Robert to dismiss such pompous thoughts. *Okay, so I find her attractive. That means nothing except that she's a pleasant traveling companion.*

Fortunately, Pen interrupted his thoughts before he had to admit to himself that he still indulged in a little deception.

"I don't want to fly if we have to leave Sydney." She leaned forward to pat the woman's arm. "Can we stay with you, Sydney?"

"Of course you can, sweetie. But I don't want you to be frightened."

"I won't be. You'll drive good," the child assured her.

Robert added a hearty, "Of course she will." What he really wanted to do was touch her, as Penelope had done. But he didn't dare.

Apparently feeling the situation was settled, Penelope leaned back against the pillows on the bed. Robert relaxed in the seat, glad his daughter had made the choice she had.

"There's a small airport in the next town," Sydney said quietly, leaning toward him.

He frowned. "Didn't you hear Pen? She wants to stay with you. And you agreed."

"Of course I agreed. But you might have doubts again about...about my driving or...or about staying with me after what you heard this afternoon."

Because of the accident, he'd almost forgotten the threat she'd received—the one that caused him to lie about their engagement. Did she think him a coward? "No, I have no doubts." He snuck a glance at her. "How long have you been receiving such messages?"

He thought at first that she wasn't going to answer. Finally, she muttered, "Since I started back driving this summer—without my dad."

After tracing her delicate features with his gaze, he said quietly, "I think you should abandon this career."

This time she didn't respond, pressing her lips tightly together, as if to hold back words she wanted to say.

"Well?" he prodded.

Her chin jutted out, stretching her slender neck, and Robert had a sudden urge to trace its length with his lips. The thought distracted him from her answer.

"What?" he said.

She repeated her words, more forcefully this time. "You deal with your problems, and I'll take care of mine."

"I have no difficulties," he assured her stoutly.

He wasn't quite lying. His problems didn't involve someone threatening him.

Unless he counted his mother.

IT WAS ALMOST EIGHT-THIRTY when they reached the restaurant where Sydney usually had dinner. Conversation had been scarce after their exchange, and Robert had even dozed a little, leaning his head against the window.

Now, as Sydney downshifted to bring the big truck to a stop, he straightened in his seat, feeling guilty. "I'm sorry. I must have fallen asleep."

"No problem," she muttered.

"But I should've driven so you could rest."

His offer didn't soften her expression. "I told you I could take care of my problems. That includes driving." Without waiting for his response, she turned to his daughter. "Penny, are you ready for dinner?"

"Yes, I'm very hungry." With a smile, Penelope scrambled from the bed, ready to go with Sydney.

"Good. We'll visit the ladies' room first and then meet your dad in the restaurant. They have great meat loaf here."

Sydney opened her door but before she could climb down, Penelope stopped her. "What's meat loaf?"

Sydney's blue eyes widened and she looked at Robert as if for help, then back at Penelope. Before Robert could speak, she said, "I didn't realize… Um, I think it's like a meat pie, only there's no pastry."

"And you like it?" Penelope asked incredulously.

For the first time in a while Sydney chuckled. "Yeah. I do."

"Then I'll have some," Penelope agreed as she took Sydney's helping hand to get out of the truck.

Robert opened his own door to follow them, deciding he, too, would have meat loaf if it made Sydney happy. He'd eat any disgusting combination of food the place offered if he could hear her laugh again.

After a brief trip to the men's room, he waited near the entrance to the restaurant, standing to one side, his cap pulled low. Only when his companions arrived did he step forward to draw the hostess's attention.

He asked for the last booth at the back.

"Sorry, the waitress for those tables is off work now. It's past the dinner hour," the gum-popping hostess explained.

"Perhaps if you share this tip with the waitress on duty, she wouldn't mind the few extra steps." He handed her a fifty-dollar bill.

With a big smile, the young woman immediately led them to the back booth. "Enjoy your meal," she said as she turned away.

"You just made a big mistake," Sydney murmured as she and Penelope slid in across from him.

"Why? Surely Americans tip servers," he said, irritated by her remark.

"Yes, but not that much. Ten dollars, maybe, for something special. But fifty dollars only calls attention to you."

"I'm sure you're quite right. I should've consulted you before I undertook such a challenging act." He regretted his sarcastic response when he saw her cheeks flush. She studied the menu, not looking at him.

"I beg your pardon," he finally said, in a low growl. "My response was rude."

"It doesn't matter," she replied politely.

But he noticed she didn't meet his gaze.

As if to underline Sydney's warning, the waitress hurried to their table and stared intently at Robert as she took their order.

To please Sydney, he handed the menus to the waitress and asked for three meat loaf dinners.

Taking the menus, the waitress scurried down the aisle to confer with the hostess.

"Are you sure I'll like meatbread?" Penelope asked Sydney.

"It's meat loaf, sweetie. And I hope so. But if you don't, we'll find something else for you to eat. It comes with mashed potatoes and peas."

"Eew, I don't like peas."

"But they're *English* peas," Sydney teased, grinning.

Robert relaxed against the back of the booth. Sydney seemed happy again. Everything would be all right. He changed his mind when he looked up and saw the waitress talking to a table of truck drivers, gesturing in their direction.

Suddenly, all four men were staring at them.

His face must've reflected his alarm.

"What's wrong?" Sydney asked, turning around to look in the truckers' direction.

"Nothing. The waitress appeared to be discussing us with those gentlemen."

"Don't worry. She's probably bragging about her tip, hoping to give them a hint."

Her words were generous, considering what had happened. He didn't like having made a mistake. Or having anyone tell him about it. Like his mother.

Or Sydney.

The waitress quickly returned with their meals, and they dug in.

"So who's Uncle Peter?" Sydney asked between bites.

Robert almost dropped his fork. "I beg your pardon?"

"Penelope said she wanted to fly to Uncle Peter's ranch."

"Oh." He carefully chewed his food, avoiding Sydney's gaze. "He's my brother."

"Why did your brother come to America?"

He frowned down at his plate. "My mother was born in Montana. My brother inherited the ranch from our grandfather."

Sydney reacted instinctively. "That's not fair! You were his grandson, too."

"You don't understand. I inherited—some other things. It was fair, I promise." He ducked his head again.

Reminding herself to be cautious, Sydney asked, "So you're going to visit your brother?"

"Yes, 'cause they're going to have a new baby," Penelope announced. "Dad's heir."

Tense silence followed. Sydney had majored in English, along with Elementary Education in college. She knew all about the rules of inheritance in England. Those rules were one of the few things she didn't like about the country.

"I think those rules stink."

This time Robert looked at her. "What rules?"

"The rules that don't allow women to inherit...things." She'd almost slipped up. Dancing around Robert's title was getting ridiculous.

Abruptly she changed the subject.

"If you're finished, we can take a shower here so that Penny's ready for bed," Sydney suggested as everyone finished.

"Take a bath in the restaurant?" Penelope asked, her eyes widening as she looked around.

"They have places for showers next to the restrooms, Penny. We could go out to the truck and get some fresh clothes and then clean up."

"That's quite a good idea, Sydney. Do you mind helping Penelope?" Robert asked. He knew he was imposing on her, but he had no choice.

"Of course not." She slid from the booth as the waitress returned, offering to fetch them dessert.

"No, thank you. If you'll bring the bill, we'll be on our way," he assured her, keeping his head down.

The woman whipped a ticket from her apron and handed it to him. "Pay at the counter, and come back to see us real soon."

He nodded, ignoring her beaming smile, then picked up the ticket, and sent the two ladies to the truck, assuring them he would follow after he settled the bill.

When he had escaped the lights of the restaurant, he breathed a sigh of relief. The waitress and hostess had stared at him the entire time at the register.

Back at the truck, he discovered Penelope digging through one of their pieces of luggage. "Dad, shall I get you out a pair of underpants, too?" She held out a pair of boxers.

"I'll get my own things, Pen." He snatched them from her hand and avoided looking at Sydney. It seemed to be his night for embarrassment. "It's time we groom ourselves. Nana would reprimand us for our disheveled appearances, poppet."

He'd meant nothing by his words, but Sydney looked away, her cheeks flaming, as if he'd implied that she, too, wouldn't pass his mother's inspection because of her appearance.

"Sydney—"

Before he could question her, or apologize—something he seemed to do a lot lately—his child interrupted. "But you said Nana always said to—"

"Never mind what I said about Nana," he said hurriedly. "Let's hurry with our ablutions so we don't put Sydney too far behind schedule."

FIFTEEN MINUTES LATER, feeling ready to face the rest of the night after his refreshing shower and shave, Robert gathered his belongings and emerged from the restaurant's shower room.

A squeal alerted him to danger.

"It *is* him!" a buxom blonde screamed and ran toward him. She was a few yards away, so his only avenue of escape was back into the shower room.

And since she was accompanied by the hostess, the waitress and three more women, he thought escape was a brilliant idea.

The room, however, left him with few options. The women were pounding on the door behind him, and there was no other exit.

THOUGH SHE'D HURRIED PENELOPE through the shower, Sydney enjoyed tending to the little girl. She was such a sweetheart, so innocent. "Now, your dad will think you're such a good girl, Penny."

"Why?"

"Because you're all scrubbed clean, like a brand-new chick."

"Dad will think I'm a chicken?" Penelope giggled.

Before Sydney could answer her, she heard a scream and then the sound of running. Holding Penelope behind her, she opened the door to the shower room.

The sight of several women pounding on the men's shower door surprised her. Until she realized what had happened.

"What are those ladies doing?" Penelope asked.

"Stay close to me." Sydney gathered their belongings and coming out into the hall, asked the women what they were after.

"The duke is in there!" one of them shouted.

"Don't tell her. He's ours!" another said.

"I heard about him. But I've got my own man. You can keep some old duke." She tried to keep her voice casual as she turned to walk away, pulling a protesting Penelope behind her.

"Honey, this one's rich and has a title. You're not thinking," the first woman assured her before she was shushed by the others.

Sydney continued on to the front door. Once they were out the door, she whispered to Penelope, "Run." They raced to the truck and she shoved Penelope up to the cab ahead of her. "Stay here, sweetie, and don't open the door to anyone."

"You're going to save Dad?" Penelope asked, her eyes filled with anxiety.

"I promise, sweetie. Lock the door." Sydney scrambled down and ran back to the restaurant, stopping to compose herself. Then she swung open the door, assuming an air of curious interest.

"Hey, did the duke have a red cap on?" she called to the women still at the shower door.

A well-built blonde turned and stared at her. "No, he didn't. What's it to you, anyway?"

"Yes, he did!" the waitress screamed before Sydney could answer. "Why?"

"I saw a man running across the parking lot to a car parked over there," Sydney replied, pointing to the opposite side of the parking lot from her truck. "There must be a back exit to the shower room."

It was a long shot, because the waitress and hostess should've known there was no exit, but the mass hysteria affecting the women seemed to erase any rational thought. Fortunately for Robert.

Screaming, they almost trampled Sydney before she could press herself against the wall.

As soon as the women were out the front door, she leaned against the door. "My lord Duke? Come out, come out, wherever you are."

Chapter Six

Sydney and Robert rode in tense silence. Since Penelope had fallen asleep half an hour ago, neither had spoken a word.

Finally, Sydney could stand the tension no longer. "For heaven's sake, loosen up. So you're a duke. Big deal." She couldn't resist grinning at him.

"Sydney, I'm sure it's a case of mistaken identity. I must look like this man. You told Carl this morning that everyone has a twin—"

"How about if I stop at the next crossroads and you and Penny can get out and thumb your way to Montana with someone who won't mind if you keep lying to them?"

He sat stiffly beside her, anger emanating from him like rain from a thundercloud. "If you're not willing to carry us any farther, that will be agreeable," he finally said, his voice hoarse.

Irrational anger roared through her. "How dare you even think of putting Penelope at such risk just to protect your stupid identity! Didn't you hear me, you jerk? Your ego may not believe it, but I *don't* want to marry you!''

Stark silence greeted Sydney's statement.

She chanced a look at her companion, then shifted her gaze back to the road.

"How did you know?"

She sighed with disgust. "I've known you were the duke since breakfast this morning." When he didn't respond, she added, "I haven't attacked you yet, have I? Or asked you to marry me?"

"You didn't have to. I offered." There was no teasing in his words, no friendship. Just wariness, as if he were looking for a trap.

Anger filled her again. They'd spent twenty-four hours together and she'd thought—hoped—they'd started a friendship, however brief it might last.

But friends trusted each other. Obviously she had expected too much. She released her anger with a deep sigh.

With an attempt at nonchalance, she said, "Don't worry. I know you didn't mean it."

ROBERT SHOULD'VE BEEN RELIEVED at her words. He should've been pleased that she had no intention of trapping him into marriage. Instead, he felt as if she'd slapped him in the face.

"You don't have to be so adamant about it," he muttered, glaring at her.

She turned to stare at him. Before she looked back at the road, he noted a smile teasing one corner of her mouth—a mouth he was entirely too interested in.

"What is so humorous?"

"Men."

Her succinct answer didn't satisfy his curiosity. "You're lumping me with all mankind?"

Her smile turned into a chuckle.

"I should've known you were of the aristocracy at once, even before I saw the picture. But most men are arrogant, so I thought it was normal."

"I resent those words," he growled, incensed.

"And I resent the fact that you didn't trust me even though we've shared the past twenty-four hours."

This time there was no humor in her voice, only a quiet hurt that twisted his gut. He should've trusted her, of course. Except he didn't trust any woman.

Especially not when his thinking was clouded with a sexual hunger that kept surprising him.

"I don't trust women." He shrugged his shoulders, unable to say more.

"And I don't trust men. So we know where we stand."

Silence filled the cab, broken only by the sound of the big tires eating up the miles of pavement. The lights from the dashboard provided a faint glow. Robert watched Sydney's face, but she kept her gaze fixed on the road.

His mind reviewed the time they'd spent together. Suddenly, he straightened in his seat. "But you did trust me! Otherwise, why did you let me come with you?''

He thought he'd scored a point.

She immediately proved him wrong. "I let you come for the same reason you trusted me enough to come along.''

"What are you talking about?"

"Penelope.''

He couldn't argue that point with her. Sitting in the darkness, feeling cloaked from her view, he asked, "Why *aren't* you interested in marrying me?"

Again she laughed. "You *want* me to trap you into marriage? Do you secretly want to marry, but can't swallow your pride?"

"You're finding this discussion quite humorous, aren't you?" Irritation filled him.

"Well, it is funny that you would fear I'd trap you into marriage, and then complain because I'm *not* trapping you into marriage. Perhaps you should make up your mind. I could turn around and take you back to that truck stop. Several of the women would be happy to accommodate you.''

"Don't be ridiculous!"

"Just make up your mind what you want.''

"I want an answer to my question," he snapped.

"Which question?"

He didn't have to see her face. He knew she was attempting to avoid answering any personal questions. Maybe he didn't have the right to ask, but he needed to know. "I want to know why you're not interested in marriage.''

"I didn't say I wasn't."

"Ah, so it's a personal aversion to me?" He tried to keep the outrage—the ridiculous hurt—out of his voice.

Again she laughed. "Of course not, Robert. We both know you're an attractive man. Half the women in America are chasing you."

"They're chasing a title, a bank balance, not me." Again he hoped he hid his emotions, because relief had filled him that she found him attractive.

"But if you were actually wanting to marry, you could let a woman draw close to you, get to know more than your bank balance or your title." Her words were softly spoken, but very much to the point.

"Why are we talking about my desire to marry? I wanted to know about *your* interest in the institution."

Somehow she twisted the conversation back to him every time.

"I have none." Her brief statement didn't give any explanation.

"You're an attractive young woman. Why aren't you planning on marriage, a family?" Attractive? That was an understatement. Her physical appearance alone would draw men. But the sweetness of her, the courage, the generosity, would all make her a wonderful wife and mother.

She continued driving as if they weren't even having a discussion.

"Sydney?"

With a sigh, she said, "I told you earlier. I don't trust men."

"Because of the pervert on the radio?"

She shook her head, a movement he barely caught in the darkness.

"Then why?"

"Why don't you trust women?"

Okay, so he was asking for openness from her when he hadn't been open himself. "I've been married. My wife was all sweetness and light until the marriage vows were spoken. Then she showed her true colors. After our child was born, she gave up any pretense. Shopping and her lover dominated her life. She ignored both me and our child."

"So she ran off with another man?"

"Not a chance. She wasn't about to give up all the lovely lolly—I mean, money. No, she was killed in a car accident. Otherwise, we'd still be married and I'd be miserable."

"You could've divorced her."

"Dukes don't divorce."

"I've heard of some nobility divorcing," she insisted, stubbornly rejecting the picture of him trapped in a deplorable marriage.

"The dukes of Hereford don't. Ask my mother."

"Does she dictate your life?"

Robert sighed and gave her a resigned grin. "No. In fact, she tries, but generally I go my own way. But in certain things, well, she's right. There's never been a divorce in the family. I kept thinking if I gave

Celia a little more time...if I were patient...I was a fool. But I can't blame my mother.''

"I don't think it's ever foolish to try to hold your family together," she whispered.

Robert studied her, his gaze roaming her slender body, her sweet face. He'd been with her a little over a day and felt he knew her better than he'd ever known his wife. And found more to admire in her, too.

Celia had been attractive, but when he'd discovered her cold nature, even sex with her had held no appeal. Sydney, on the other hand, could arouse him with her smile. He hated to think what a conflagration she'd start with her touch.

"I guess that explains your reluctance to marry again," Sydney said. "I'm sorry I was angry earlier. I just don't like being lied to."

Robert's story of betrayal touched Sydney more than she wanted it to. The arrogant man beside her didn't need her to feel sympathy for him. He had too many people attending to his needs.

His physical needs.

She immediately slammed that thought out of her mind. His needs, of any kind, were not her business.

"Now it's your turn." Robert looked at her expectantly.

Had he thrown her that bone of a confession to force her to open up? Her jaw firmed. "I have nothing to say."

"That's not fair."

No, it wasn't. Much as she hated to admit it, her father had raised her to be fair.

"Fine. I was engaged to marry. When my father died, my fiancé moved on."

Her brief story was met with silence.

Then, out of the darkness, came one word. "Why?"

She gave up with a sigh. After all, it was her fault. She should never have said anything. "I have financial obligations that he didn't want to shoulder."

"Money? He left you because of money?"

The incredulity in his voice was satisfying—until she remembered that he had probably never experienced a lack of money.

"When you don't have much money, it seems more important." She didn't like defending Andrew, but she'd accepted his behavior a long time ago.

After an extended silence, Robert said, "Well, it appears we both have good reason not to ever consider marriage again."

DID SHE DARE?

It was almost midnight and she was too tired to continue driving. But it wasn't her exhaustion that tempted her.

It was Robert. After their revealing conversation, she found herself more drawn to him than ever. Not a good thing.

It wasn't just his sexy body, his air of command, his offer to protect her. No, it was the broken heart he hid beneath all that terrific packaging. They had something in common, after all.

As she stared at her companion, slumped against the passenger's seat, she debated again the thought that had passed through her head over the last two hours. He'd been sleeping in fits, waking because of his discomfort, twisting and turning to find a more comfortable position.

It seemed the only humane thing to do.

"Robert? Wake up. I'm stopping now."

"It's time to get up?" he asked in confusion, staring around him in the darkness.

"No, it's time to get some sleep."

"But I *was* sleeping," he protested.

"We're going to get in bed now. I mean, I think the three of us—with Penny in the middle—can share the bed. That way we'll all get some rest." And Sydney wouldn't have a guilty conscience.

"We're going to bed together?"

Just the thought brought a heat to her cheeks. She was glad he couldn't see the color in the dark.

"With Penny," she emphasized as she slid out of the seat she'd been in for too many hours. "We can both sleep in our clothes, or...or you can put on some shorts and a T-shirt, if you want."

"Okay."

"You should get in bed first, against the wall. That way I might be able to start up in the morning without waking you. Try not to wake Penny when you crawl over her."

Was that subtle enough? She'd already spelled out

the fact that they would keep Penelope between them, hadn't she?

She tried again. "I'll wait here until you're settled in. Just call me when you're ready." She held back the curtain and waited.

Still looking confused, Robert got up and ducked past her. She let the curtain drop and stood there in the dark, listening as he switched on the wall lamp and opened a suitcase. Finally, after several minutes, she whispered, "Are you in bed yet?"

"Uh, yes, I'm, uh, quite settled in."

Then why hadn't he called her, as she'd asked? Had he planned on letting her stand up the rest of the night, she wondered grouchily. She went past the curtain, reaching up to turn off the lamp, before sitting on the edge of the bed to take off her sneakers.

"Are you sure you'll have enough room?" he whispered in the dark.

She'd been trying to pretend he wasn't there. She hadn't looked across the mattress before she shrouded them in darkness. Her struggle probably wouldn't have worked anyway, but his voice filling the space made sure of it.

"It's fine. Good night."

"Good night. And thank you."

It was no big deal, she assured herself. After all, he'd slept in the seat last night and gotten very little rest. It was only fair.

Too bad *she* wasn't going to get more sleep. She'd never relax knowing that Robert was a mere two feet from her.

ROBERT WAS USED to sleeping alone.

But the warmth that surrounded him as he began to awaken the next morning was caused by another warm body. A woman was pressed against him, her breasts touching his chest, her legs stretched out under one of his. The scent of her, and her head on his shoulder, made him smile as he slowly awoke.

Maybe we'll make love again before breakfast. He rubbed his cheek against her silky hair as he wrapped an arm around her, pressing her more tightly against him. His body was responding rapidly.

Without conscious thought, his lips traced down her face to find her lips—lips that he craved. He'd been wanting to kiss those lips ever since he'd found her.

As he reached his goal, discovering the perfect fit he'd already imagined, something about his thoughts began to irritate, to tease. But that notion disappeared as sensations filled him—wonderful, glorious sensations that he hadn't felt in a long time. Or maybe never.

Her arms went around his neck as she opened to him. His need grew and became more urgent. One hand slipped beneath the shirt she was wearing and he felt her bare skin, sending frissons of desire through him.

Penelope must be playing nearby. Her childish voice was humming in the background. He hoped the door was closed because he didn't want—

Reality intruded.

Robert opened his eyes only a second before Sydney opened hers. They sprang apart in shock.

"Oh, no!" she gasped, scrambling to the edge of the bed. "What— Where's Penny?"

"I'm here," a tiny voice said behind her. "I was drawing in the front seat."

"I— What time is it?"

Robert stared as she checked her wristwatch. He didn't bother to look at his own.

"Oh, no! It's almost eight o'clock!" She shoved her feet into her shoes and automatically began re-braiding her hair.

Before he could think of anything to say, she had slipped into her seat and started up the engine. Within thirty seconds, they were on the road.

"Aren't you going to get up, Dad?" Penelope asked, watching him curiously now that the curtain had been pushed back.

Robert knew he was in no state to show himself to the females just now. "No, Pen, I'm going to wait for a few minutes. You sit with Sydney and fasten your seat belt."

"Okay," she agreed with a smile. "But my tummy is empty. When are we going to eat breakfast?"

They'd bought some groceries after their meal last night, so Robert felt safe in promising, "I'll find you something in a few minutes."

As soon as the bulge in his pants disappeared. As soon as he could erase the memory of the feel of

Sydney in his arms. As soon as he could forget his dreams.

SYDNEY STARED BLINDLY at the road, grateful for the lack of traffic this morning. Not only was she behind schedule, but she was embarrassed. Embarrassed? She would be shamed for life. After assuring Robert she had no interest in him, she'd ended up in his arms.

What had happened? She'd fallen asleep clinging to her side of the bed, with Penny safely between them. But the child must've slipped out of bed early.

Had she, Sydney, turned to the man the moment his daughter was gone? How long had she been in his arms? In spite of her embarrassment, there was a longing deep within her to remember.

What little she could recall had been heavenly.

"Don't!" she snapped.

"I didn't do anything, Sydney," Penelope assured her, her eyes anxious.

"Not you, sweetie. I was…was talking to myself. See if your dad is ready to pour you some milk. I think those oatmeal cookies we bought will make an excellent breakfast."

"Yummy! Biscuits for breakfast. Nana never lets me have biscuits for breakfast." Penelope unfastened her seat belt and went to the curtain. "Dad?"

"Uh, yeah, I heard. I'll be right there."

"You and your dad might want to sit on the bed to eat your breakfast. There's not much room up here." And that would give her a few more minutes

before she had to face him. Did he now think she
had intended to trap him all along? Her cheeks
flamed with color.

She heard him push back the curtain behind her,
but she didn't look over her shoulder or even glance
in the rearview mirror. Instead, she drove as if she
were in downtown Chicago, surrounded by crazy
drivers.

"Do we have cups?"

She risked looking in the mirror and found his
cheeks as red as her own. "In the other closet in a
box on the floor."

The sounds of the two of them rounding up the
necessities eased her tension a little. Maybe he
wouldn't remember their kiss. He might think it was
a dream. She'd keep her fingers crossed. If he didn't
mention it, she could pretend that it was a dream.

"You have a telly?" Penelope asked, moving to
stand beside her.

"A telly? Oh, the television. Yes, I'd forgotten
about it. Did you want to watch it?" She carried a
small portable television that she could plug into an
outlet by the bed.

"Yes! There are some jolly good cartoons on it. I
saw them in New York."

"Your father might not—"

Robert interrupted. "I don't mind. Where do I
plug it in?"

She told him and sent up a silent prayer, hoping
that Robert was as addicted to cartoons as was his
daughter.

"Don't spill your milk," Robert warned Penelope, and Sydney risked another glance in the mirror, only to find him turned to look at her.

"Ready for breakfast?"

"Me?" she said, gulping.

"Yes. Do you want milk with your biscuit?"

"Yes, please." *Concentrate on your driving.*

A strong tanned forearm came into her line of vision, putting a glass of milk in the cup holder. Immediately, memories of his hand sliding beneath her shirt made breathing difficult.

This is ridiculous, Sydney. You've had a man touch you before. But not the way Robert had.

He put a cookie wrapped in a napkin on the flat part of the dashboard, then settled into the seat beside her.

"Don't you want to watch cartoons?"

"No."

He didn't have a glass of milk, but he held a cookie. "Don't you want something to drink?"

"Yes. Do you have a pot of coffee hidden that I don't know about?" His deep voice was gravelly, as if he were still half asleep.

"Sorry, no. And I can't afford to stop until I have to fuel. Which will be in a couple of hours."

"Hmmph. Guess I'll have to wait."

"You could try a soda. It'll have caffeine."

"For breakfast?"

His outraged voice drew a quick glance.

"It was just a suggestion." And one she intended to follow when she finished her cookie and milk. But she had no intention of trying to convince him. In fact, she'd prefer not to exchange any more conversation with him until memories of their closeness faded a little more.

"Sydney, we have to talk."

Chapter Seven

Robert had never before felt so awkward. But then, he'd never before tried to seduce an unwilling woman. Sydney had already told him that she had no interest in him.

That hadn't stopped him from taking advantage of her generosity—from touching her, holding her, kissing her.

Even thinking about it was bringing on another reaction. And he didn't have a cover to hide it this time.

He cleared his throat.

Sydney had said nothing. He frowned. Had she not heard him? Or was she waiting for his apology?

"I'm sorry I—" he began, only to stop as she also spoke.

"I didn't mean to attack you." Her voice was tight, almost angry.

Her words stunned him.

"You? You didn't do anything. I—"

"I didn't *intend* to do anything, but I kissed you.

I don't want you to think I was trying to trap you.'' She stared straight ahead.

He took a deep breath. If his nerves hadn't been zinging all over the place, he might've laughed. ''Sydney, *I* kissed *you.*''

''You were asleep. I was lying on your shoulder.''

''Are you saying you were awake when—before I kissed you?''

''No!'' She whipped her head around to stare at him, astonishment in her eyes. ''No, I wasn't, but—''

''Sydney, I've never worked this hard to prove I was *guilty* of something.'' This time he did chuckle, which drew a glare from her. But he was feeling much more lighthearted since he discovered she didn't blame him for their...interlude.

''Which should tell you you weren't at fault.'' Her quiet words were filled with embarrassment and sorrow.

Did she regret their touching? Had she not enjoyed— Bloody hell, ''enjoyed'' seemed a mild way to describe his feelings at finding her in his arms. ''Perhaps we should chalk it up to an accident.''

''That's generous of you.''

Exasperation filled him. ''Sydney, you act as if you committed murder. Whoever initiated the kiss, I was the one who slid my hand up— I mean, I wanted more.''

And still did. He wanted her beneath him, in his arms, begging him to take her.

That thought took his breath away.

Sydney remained silent, her cheeks flushed.

"Drink your milk," he ordered, suddenly ready to end the examination before he embarrassed himself again. He didn't know what had become of his famous control, but he'd better rediscover it soon if he was going to continue traveling with the sexy lady beside him.

SYDNEY PRESSED HER TRUCK as hard as she dared. If she didn't reach Fargo by five o'clock, she'd have to unload the truck herself.

But she also had to be wary of highway patrollers. She didn't need a ticket on her driving record.

When she stopped for fuel around ten, she asked Robert to purchase some sandwiches and drinks to get them through the day.

Again he offered to drive when they got back in the cab, but she refused.

"I thought you at least trusted me to drive," he said, watching her carefully.

"It's not a matter of trust. Driving is my job." She didn't look at him.

"My dad is a good driver," Penelope offered, her hand confidingly held in Sydney's.

"I know he is, sweetie, but I can drive. Are there still some cartoons on television?" she asked, kissing Penelope's cheek.

Robert was ashamed of the jealousy that filled him. After their awkward discussion, she had hardly acknowledged he was alive, much less touched him.

And he wanted her touch.

But he made no effort to move closer, nor to

change her mind. He was used to being in charge, to having everyone rush to meet his needs.

But he wasn't in England now. He couldn't order Sydney to do as he said. Instead, he settled Penelope with a new storybook he'd bought along with the sandwiches, then sat down and fastened his seat belt.

Sydney sent him a sharp look before turning her attention to the business of driving.

They had been traveling quietly for some time when Penelope shrieked.

Sydney immediately applied the brakes, her anxious eyes looking in the rearview mirror. Robert undid his seat belt and sprang to the bed to protect his beloved child.

Instead of needing protection, however, she was pointing to the television. "Look! It's Nana."

Sydney eased the big rig to the side of the road. "Is everything all right?"

Since the program had just gone to commercial, Robert couldn't say. "You couldn't have seen Nana on television, poppet. You must be mistaken."

Penelope frowned. "It looked like her. And she was talking about you."

Robert groaned.

Then Sydney came to stand beside him and he had difficulty concentrating on his mother. Sydney was much more tempting.

"Oh, it's the Oprah Winfrey show. Do you get her in England?"

"I don't know." He fell silent as his mother appeared on screen. Penelope had been right. Robert braced himself for disaster.

The hostess smiled at his mother. "Duchess, if your son wants a wife, why is he hiding?"

"Oh, Oprah, darling, his heart is broken," she said dramatically, placing her hand across her chest. "He's so afraid to trust. A woman will have to be very persuasive to convince him to marry again. That's why I'm appealing to the women of America to save my son. Save him from a broken heart.

"I know the women of America are spunky enough to break through the ice around his heart and teach him to love again."

"Bloody hell!" Robert muttered, shutting his eyes. "Has the woman lost her mind?"

A low chuckle made him snap open his eyes.

Sydney was staring at the television in fascination, a wide smile on her face.

"You think this is amusing?"

"Sorry," she said softly. "But look at her, Robert. She's another Sarah Bernhardt. She's having the time of her life."

"And making mine miserable."

"Thanks a lot. I didn't realize traveling with me was so terrible." She turned away so quickly that he couldn't see her face.

Leaping to the front of the truck where she'd resumed her place behind the wheel, he hurriedly apologized. "I didn't mean—"

She grinned at him as she eased the truck back on the road. "I know. I was just teasing you. You'd better get back there and find out what else she's got to say.''

He listened to his mother until the show ended. Then he returned to the front seat. Sydney was concentrating on her driving, and he kept quiet. He could only hope few people watched this "Oprah." A few miles outside Fargo, North Dakota, he finally said, "It's a quarter to five."

"I know."

"How long until we arrive?"

"Probably half an hour."

Her voice was despondent, tired.

"Will they be open to unload?"

"They'll receive the goods. I'll have to unload."

"What are you carrying?"

"Canned goods."

He said nothing else, but he determined Sydney would not do the unloading. Her slender frame had already done a man's job, driving the big rig. If he had to unload by himself, he would. But he suspected money would convince some of the workers to stay after hours.

When they reached the distribution center where the delivery was to be made, it was sixteen minutes after five. Sydney pulled past the entrance and halted, preparing to back her rig in.

Robert opened his door.

"Where are you going?" she asked, her voice ragged with exhaustion.

"To see if there's anyone around."

"I told you they wouldn't unload after five."

"I'll check. Penelope, stay on the bed out of Sydney's way." He didn't wait for either female to question him. He'd been patient long enough.

SYDNEY WATCHED HIM STRIDE across the concrete, command in every step. Too bad his being a duke wouldn't impress the men in the warehouse. She was too tired to unload the truck, but she didn't really have a choice.

It took her several tries to back the truck flush with the loading dock, but she didn't feel too badly about that. Some of the men didn't do any better. For a brief moment, she allowed herself to slump against the seat.

"Are you tired, Sydney?" Penelope asked softly.

"Yes, sweetie, I'm tired, but I haven't finished my job. Will you be all right by yourself?"

"Where are you going?"

"I have to make sure the truck is unloaded. I'll tell your dad to come keep you company." She pasted on a bright smile for the child, then opened the door and climbed down.

When she reached the back of her truck, she found the door already open and six husky men passing the boxes into the warehouse. "What's going on?"

Robert was talking to the manager and turned around when she spoke. "Kevin said it was all right even though you were a little late."

She knew something wasn't kosher. She and her dad had come in late several times and Kevin had never gone out of his way to help them.

Robert came over and took her arm, turning her back toward the truck. "Everything is settled. Go keep Pen company. Stretch out on the bed. When they've finished, we'll go find some dinner."

She looked over her shoulder and discovered Kevin and several of the other men watching them. "You paid them extra, didn't you?"

"Go."

"But, Robert, I can't afford to—"

"If you don't get in that truck and stop protesting, I'll...I'll...."

She straightened, and looked him square in the eye. "You'll what?"

"I'll kiss you again."

Something in his eyes told her he wasn't kidding. In spite of a lingering desire that lapped at her consciousness, she headed back to the cab.

"SAY, WHAT ARE YOU TO SYD?"

Robert straightened and stared down his nose at Kevin. The truck was unloaded and Kevin was paid. Just what did he want now? "A friend," he answered vaguely.

"Oh? 'Cause we heard she was engaged."

How had warehouse men in North Dakota heard about something that had occurred hundreds of miles away and had no national importance? "And?"

"We was just wondering if you were the one she's going to marry. I mean, we've all known Syd since she was a kid."

"And you were going to walk away and leave her to unload on her own?"

"Hey, she thinks she can do a man's work. No reason to cut her any slack." Kevin looked around him for corroboration, receiving nods from the men.

Robert stifled the impulse to slug Kevin and any man who backed him. He thought of the exhaustion on Sydney's face and her struggle to meet the deadline. But he also knew any altercation would upset her. "Righto."

As he turned away, Kevin called, "Nice doin' business with you. Say, we heard you were that duke looking for an American woman. That true?"

"Not a word of it." At least not the words about him looking for an American woman. He wasn't looking for any woman. And if he were, he'd already found quite an impressive one.

He swung up into the cab of the truck to find his daughter watching the interminable cartoons while Sydney, curled around her, slept.

"Shh, Dad. Sydney's sleeping."

"I can see, poppet."

"She was very tired."

"Yes, I know. But I think she should have some dinner, don't you?" He studied Sydney's sleeping form as he spoke, remembering how warm and soft she'd been this morning, lying against him.

"Me, too. I'm starving!" Penelope bounced for emphasis and her movement stirred Sydney.

Her eyes flickered open and she raised up on one elbow. "Robert?"

He would've come from the ends of the earth when she called him with that husky voice. "Yes, love, we're finished. I thought we might have dinner now."

"Okay. There are some sandwiches—"

"No. We'll go to a restaurant."

"I have to ditch the trailer. I'm leaving it here and picking it back up when I deliver the load from Denver."

Penelope, listening intently, asked, "Will the bed stay here?"

"No, sweetie. Just the trailer." She scooted to the edge of the bed and searched for her sneakers.

Robert didn't offer to drive again. He knew she'd insist on doing so. Because it was her job.

They dropped the trailer off at a shipping yard a couple of blocks away, but Robert was lost in thought.

He hated Sydney's job. He hated her having to rely on people like Kevin and Carl. Not to mention the jerk who was threatening her. If he had his way... But he didn't. And he wouldn't be around. In another month, he'd be back in England, carrying out his duties.

And Sydney would remain here.

"Are you sure you don't want to fly?" Sydney's voice broke through Robert's reverie. "I mean, with your mother on television, I think you'll be recognized wherever you go."

"I'd rather we keep going, if you don't mind." He held his breath, waiting for her response. He didn't want to delve too deeply into his feelings, but he knew he didn't want to leave Sydney. Not yet.

"I don't mind. I was only thinking of you."

"Actually I'm hoping no one saw the program."

No one see Oprah? Sydney smiled. Yeah. No one except several million people.

"Now, where shall we eat tonight?" he said. "My treat."

"No, I think I should pay. After all, you arranged for the workers to stay overtime. If you'll tell me how much you paid, I can—"

"You'll do no such thing. Now, I'm starving. I think I feel like a steak. I haven't had one in a while, what with the mad cow disease in England. You don't have that over here, do you?"

"No. And I know just the place." A few minutes later she parked next to a nice-looking restaurant. "Perhaps you and Penelope should eat without me," she said, looking down at herself. "I'm pretty bedraggled."

For the first time since he'd awakened with her in his arms that morning, he touched her, reaching over to tuck a stray hair behind her ear. "You look perfect. Come along."

"And if they don't want me there, you'll just offer extra money?" she challenged, raising her chin.

"Sydney, if you're looking for a fight, go back to the warehouse. All I want is dinner. Ready, Penelope?"

"Yes, but I need to go before dinner."

"Ah. That's Sydney's department. See if she'll

come along with us.'' He shot Sydney a questioning look, as if her presence at dinner meant nothing to him.

"That's dirty pool, Robert." She rubbed her forehead. "Should I be calling you Duke or something?"

"Not unless you want to get revenge on me, like my mother," he said, a rueful smile on his face. "Why don't we just go eat." This time he got no argument from either lady.

When they were finally seated in the restaurant and had given their orders to the waitress, Robert decided he should launch his next plan. "I think we should stay at a hotel tonight."

"Of course," Sydney agreed at once. "I can drop you off at whatever hotel you like."

"I meant all three of us."

"No, that's not necessary. I have the bed in the truck."

"I think we deserve a treat. And we want to share it with you." He didn't want her sleeping alone, unprotected, and he didn't dare share the bed with her again—Penelope or no Penelope.

"We could watch a big telly, Sydney, together. It would be fun," Penelope added. "And they have room service. You just call and tell someone what you want to eat, and they bring it."

"And they have hot showers that aren't in truck stops," Robert added with a grin.

"It's an unnecessary expense," she said, looking away even as she shook her head.

"Did you and your dad never stay in a hotel?"

"Sometimes we...we stayed at a bed-and-breakfast here in Fargo, but—"

"Then we'll stay there."

"I didn't make a reservation. They might be full."

"Give me the number and I'll call."

"No, I— All right, I'll go call."

"You'll come back?" he asked, suddenly afraid to let her out of his sight. Her look of surprise reassured him.

"Of course I'll come back. I just ordered a steak, didn't I?"

NOW SHE COULD ADMIT IT: she couldn't—didn't—dare to share the truck bed with Robert again. The desire to crawl up in his arms and never let go of him again was so tempting that she was afraid she'd give in to such a ridiculous idea even in her sleep. She couldn't be trusted.

She had no choice really.

"Mrs. Wright? This is Sydney Thomas."

The elderly lady's response was heartwarming. After Sydney answered several questions about how she was doing, she asked about the availability of rooms.

"A'course I got a room for you, honey. Are you bringing your fiancé with you?"

Sydney gasped. "No, Mrs. Wright, not my fiancé. But we'll need two rooms, one double and one single. I have a couple of passengers with me."

"But I heard you was engaged to some duke."

"Oh, you know how gossip is."

Much to her relief, Mrs. Wright stopped her questions. Sydney told her they would be there in an hour or two, after dinner, and hung up the phone.

Sydney realized she had to warn Robert. Now he actually might prefer to fly on to his brother's ranch. But just thinking about his leaving made her want to crawl into a corner and cry.

Straightening her shoulders and donning a smile, she returned to the table to discover that iced tea and a salad had been delivered for each of them. Robert and Penelope were politely waiting for her return before eating.

"I'm sorry. I didn't know you would wait."

"Nana says—" Penelope began.

"Yes, Pen, we know. Now that Sydney has returned, you may eat."

Robert sent Sydney a warm smile as Penelope began eating her salad. Sydney sighed, then caught herself. She would miss him more than she'd ever thought possible. Penelope, too.

"Um, I got us rooms, but I'm afraid I have some bad news."

"There's only one bed?" Robert asked.

"No!" Sydney almost shouted, and promptly dropped the fork she'd just picked up.

Robert immediately summoned the waitress to fetch her a clean fork. "Then what's the bad news?"

"The word has already reached Fargo that we're...we're engaged. And that you may be the Duke of Hereford."

"Is that all? I already knew that."

He calmly began eating, but Sydney stared at him, her mouth hanging open. "You knew? How?"

"That chap Kevin. He insisted on informing me."

"But what are you going to do?"

He smiled at her. "First, I'm going to eat my steak. But they won't bring it until you eat your salad. So do you think you might manage a few bites?"

"Yes, but—"

"The salad?"

"I'm almost finished with mine, Dad," Penelope said, shoving her bowl toward him. "Do I have to eat any more?"

"Hmmm. Do you promise to eat some steak and potato?"

"Yes. And then we can have dessert, okay?"

"We'll see how much you eat."

"You sound just like Nana."

Sydney listened to their exchange, a bewildered look on her face. They were pretending everything was normal. But it wasn't.

"Robert—"

"Quit worrying, love. No one seems the least bit interested in me here. And I doubt there will be enough people at the bed-and-breakfast to matter."

"No, Mrs. Wright said she didn't have any boarders this evening. We'll be the only ones."

"Then, see? We'll have an uninterrupted evening and get some rest. Then tomorrow, we'll head for Montana."

It sounded like heaven to Sydney, but she still

wasn't sure. After all, those women at the truck stop hadn't seemed too uninterested.

By the time Penelope was eating her ice cream, Sydney felt more relaxed. It seemed Robert was right. In Fargo, no one cared that he was a duke.

Or did they?

"Lord Hereford?"

They looked up at a seductive blonde who suddenly appeared at their table.

"I'm Kitty Dutton. And I've got a lot to offer you."

Since she began unbuttoning the snug sweater she wore, no one was left in any doubt about her intentions.

"You know, Sydney," Robert said calmly, "I do believe they have that lady Oprah on the telly here in Fargo."

Chapter Eight

Sydney, not Robert, leaped to her feet to protest. "You're not going to strip here in front of everyone, are you?"

"Why not? I'm proud of my body. And I can't expect the duke to be interested without knowing what he's getting."

That last line was delivered with a smile that set Sydney's teeth on edge. Had the woman no shame? And the even more urgent question, would Robert want to see what the brazen woman was offering? Sydney turned to look at him.

"Whatever you have to show, madam," he said in a bored tone, "I'm not interested."

"But I'm much better looking than her," the blonde snapped, throwing her hand toward Sydney.

Robert lost his bored look as he turned to Sydney. The warmth in his smile reached her as he said, "You don't even begin to compare. Waitress? Our check, please."

The altercation had drawn a lot of attention, and Sydney was as eager as Robert was to escape the public place. But her distaste for the woman's actions was tempered by the pleasure that filled her at Robert's praise.

Word spread quickly, and several women approached them as they headed for the door.

Sydney's ears burned as she heard the offers the women made. She was embarrassed for her fellow American women. How could a title, or money for that matter, make so many women lose their pride? She might be able understand their determination if they'd spent any time with him, the way she had.

Not that she would—

"I think a fast escape is called for," Robert whispered as he swung Penelope up into his arms. "Got your keys ready?"

"Yes," she said and rushed out the door.

"Wait!" a woman called. "I want to—"

Sydney didn't care what the woman wanted— what any of them wanted. And apparently neither did Robert, since he was close on her heels.

Once they were in the cab and she was driving out of the parking lot, Robert suggested she not drive straight to the bed-and-breakfast.

"Why not?"

"Because I'm afraid we might be followed."

She shot him a quick look and then did as he suggested.

Penelope, in the front seat with her dad, frowned, looking puzzled. "What was that lady going to show you, Dad? Did she have a puppy or something?"

"A puppy?" Sydney said with a startled laugh.

"Not exactly, poppet."

"Then what did she want to show you?"

Robert seemed to have no answer ready. He stared at Sydney. With a grin, much to her own surprise, she said, "The lady wanted to show your dad how pretty she was."

Penelope frowned again. "I think you're lots prettier, Sydney. Don't you, Dad?"

"Absolutely, my dear. Sydney is quite beautiful."

"I'm not," Sydney protested automatically.

"Of course you are, Sydney," Penelope said, reaching out to smooth Sydney's braid. "And you look like a princess when your hair isn't braided. What's that one in my book, Dad?"

Robert grinned at Sydney as he answered his daughter. "I think you're talking about Rapunzel."

"Yes, that's her," Penelope agreed, clapping her hands.

"I'll tell you something even more impressive about Sydney," Robert began, still staring at her.

Sydney knew they were being nice, but she couldn't have asked him to stop even if she'd wanted to. She had to know what he was going to say.

"The most impressive thing about Sydney is her heart. She's kinder than anyone I've ever met."

"Yeah! That's why she gives good hugs, like a real mum!" Penelope agreed with a cheer.

Sydney liked hearing those words. Too much so, in fact. But they reminded her that she'd be alone soon enough. Time to change the subject. "Are we being followed?"

Robert had been watching the road behind them in the rearview mirror on his side of the truck. "I'm afraid so. Do you think you can lose them?"

"I'll try."

She headed for the outskirts of town where she could go faster. They could double back later. When she turned onto the main road, Interstate 94, and pressed on the gas pedal, she breathed a sigh of relief.

A siren followed immediately, and her gut tightened. "Is he after me?"

"I'm afraid so, Sydney."

She eased to the side of the road, saying nothing. This ticket would be the first blemish on her driving record. She felt almost sick to her stomach.

After coming to a halt, she opened her door and climbed down. Until she heard the slam of the opposite door, she didn't know that Robert was also getting out to join her. She rounded the back of her rig, complaining, "Robert, I can handle—"

"Good evening, folks." The deep voice of the highway patroller snagged her attention.

"Good evening," she said, her voice catching in her throat.

"Officer, this incident is my mistake," Robert said at once.

"Robert, I said I could handle this," Sydney protested.

"You know it's my fault, Sydney. I want to explain to the officer."

"You can't—"

"Excuse me," the officer interrupted, his voice filled with dry amusement. "If both of you could talk to me, instead of each other, we might make more progress."

They both started talking at once and the officer motioned for silence again. Then he turned to Robert. "Since you're so eager to explain, you go first."

"Thank you, officer. I'm the Duke of Hereford."

It took a moment for the officer to make the connection.

"You mean the one in the newspaper looking for a wife?"

"That's me. That is, I'm the Duke of Hereford. It is my mother's imagination that I'm seeking a wife."

The officer chuckled. "I know what you mean. I have a mother trying to marry me off, too."

"Could we discuss my speeding?" Sydney demanded, her voice cold.

The officer raised his eyebrows and Robert spoke again. "We've just had an unfortunate experience at the restaurant where we were dining. A young woman recognized me and offered to, um, remove her clothing to show me her assets."

"Wow! That must've—" he caught Sydney's glare out of the corner of his eye and cleared his throat "—been embarrassing."

"Yes. I suggested Sydney try to lose the women who followed us from the restaurant. We've driven a long way today and I'd like to have an uninterrupted night."

When the officer gave Sydney the once-over in a

not-too-subtle appraisal, she felt her cheeks get hot.
The officer must have thought she and Robert would
be sharing that uninterrupted night. She started to
correct his impression, but decided to remain silent.
To protest would only have called attention to their
situation.

"Well, I can surely understand your problem.
Maybe I've scared them away for you. Why don't
you go on to your hotel? Just don't be speeding anymore. Right, little lady?" He grinned at her, as if
they shared a secret.

"Right," she snapped and turned on her heel.

She heard Robert express his gratitude, something
she should've done, but she couldn't speak without
fearing she'd lose control. Little lady, indeed!

Robert climbed into the cab, a grin on his face.

"Nice chap, wasn't he?"

"He thought we were—" She stopped abruptly,
noting Penelope's interested stare. "Never mind."

Robert gave her a considering look, but he said
mildly, "Let's go to the bed-and-breakfast. We're all
tired."

"Will they have room service?" Penelope asked.

"No, they won't. But you couldn't possibly be
hungry, poppet. Not after your big dinner."

"But I didn't get to finish my ice cream," the
child complained.

"We'll get some more ice cream tomorrow." He
turned his gaze to Sydney and she shivered. "Sydney
won't be on a tight schedule tomorrow. I'm sure we
can convince her to stop."

"Okay, Dad. May I stay with Sydney tonight?"

"Would you mind sharing your room, Sydney?"

She understood the question, but Sydney was so tired she couldn't shut out the immediate image of Robert rather than Penelope in her bed. Demurely, she nodded in agreement, but said nothing.

"Lucky you, Pen. Sydney says it's okay."

SYDNEY PARKED HER RIG behind the bed-and-breakfast. If, as Mrs. Wright had earlier said, they were the only boarders, perhaps their stay would go unnoticed by the rest of Fargo. She sincerely hoped so. If Robert had been facing such incredible pursuit before he hooked up with her, she could understand his decision to keep his identity secret.

"Come right in, Sydney," Mrs. Wright said with a big smile and a hug. "My, it's nice to see you again. I was so sorry to hear about your father's death last fall."

"Thank you, Mrs. Wright. This is Robert..." she paused, wondering what name she should give.

Robert stepped forward. "Robert Morris, Mrs. Wright. And this is my daughter, Penelope."

"Ooh, what a lovely accent. And such nice manners. Are you the duke everyone is talking about?"

The lady's avid expression gave Sydney pause, but Robert seemed to have no qualms about revealing his identity to her.

"Yes, I'm the Duke of Hereford, but I hope you will, as the Americans say, keep that information under your hat."

"Well, of course I will. Are a lot of women chasing you?"

"Yes."

"But Sydney's caught you. She's a wonderful girl."

Sydney opened her mouth to protest Mrs. Wright's assumption, but Robert spoke before she could.

"Yes, she is."

"Um, do you have our rooms ready? We're really tired." Not only was she tired, but Sydney also felt her control was slipping when it came to resisting Robert's charm. After spending the last forty-eight hours with the man, she could use a break to work on her resistance.

"Of course I do. Follow me." Then she stopped. "Don't you have any luggage?"

"Yes," Robert assured her. "It's in the truck. I'll bring it in later."

The rooms she showed them were next door to each other, opposite a shared hall bath.

"Now, if you just want to pay for one room, I've got a cot I can set up for the little one," Mrs. Wright offered, smiling at Robert. "I know engaged couples anticipate their wedding vows these days."

Though Sydney blushed, Robert appeared to accept the lady's offer with composure.

"Thank you for your understanding, madam, but Penelope and Sydney will take one room, and I will take the other."

"A perfect gentleman. Your dad would be proud, Syd," Mrs. Wright commented with a smile.

Unable to trust herself to say anything, Sydney managed an awkward bob of her head, then turned to Penelope. "Which room shall we take, Pen?"

"The pink one. It looks all girlie. You like the green room, don't you, Dad?" she asked, turning to her father.

"Of course, Pen. You hop in the tub for your bath while I bring in the luggage."

"But it's early yet, Dad. See, it's still light outside."

"After your bath, we can lie in bed and watch television together," Sydney suggested, hoping to avert an argument.

Penelope liked her suggestion and immediately turned to the bathroom, pulling Sydney by the hand.

Before the two of them could close the door behind them, Sydney heard Mrs. Wright say, "A natural-born mother. You are so lucky, Duke."

Penelope shut the door before Sydney could hear Robert's response.

PENELOPE SWISHED THE WATER around her in the tub, her thoughts on recent events. "Sydney?"

"Yes, Penny?"

"Why was that lady going to take off her clothes? I thought ladies put on clothes to make them look pretty." She watched carefully as Sydney considered the question.

"Um, well, ladies should dress in pretty things to look nice, but...uh, some ladies are afraid they won't be pretty enough, so they try something different. But Nana would tell you that nice ladies don't do that.''

"You're a nice lady.''

Sydney was touched. "Why, thank you, Penny. I hope so.'' She began putting cream on her face.

"Do you have pretty clothes to dress in?''

"I have a few at home, but I don't need pretty clothes when I'm driving. They just take up room.''

"But how will you look pretty for men?''

Sydney cleared her throat. "Um, I'm working right now, Penny. I don't have time to dress for men.''

"Oh.'' She swirled her finger in the water, making designs. "But I thought you said you *weren't* working now. Didn't you?''

"Yes, that's right, for a couple of days, but I don't have anything with me but jeans and T-shirts. Sorry if I don't look pretty enough.'' She smiled, which relieved Penelope. She wouldn't want to hurt her friend's feelings.

"Oh, you look pretty enough for me. I meant you should dress up for Dad.''

"Um, no, Penny, I….'' Sydney stopped and swallowed. "Time to get out of the tub, sweetie. Your dad is probably waiting for the bathroom.''

WHEN ROBERT CAME OUT of the bathroom after a hot shower that restored a little energy, he passed by the ladies' room with an envious look at the closed door. After storing his dirty clothes and toiletries in his suitcase, he picked up a map, returned to the closed door, and rapped softly.

He heard a scrambling, and then Sydney's voice quietly asked, "Who is it?"

"It's me. Robert. May I come in?"

The door swung open to reveal a freshly-scrubbed Sydney, her face as innocent as Penelope's. Her hair was hanging unbraided to her waist, a dark red curtain that tempted him.

"Is something wrong?"

"No, Rapunzel, but I thought we should discuss tomorrow's travel plans."

"Penny is already asleep. I'm afraid we'll wake her. Tomorrow—"

"Come to my room," he suggested.

She reacted as if he'd invited her to a seduction, her eyes widening in surprise and consternation.

"It won't take long. We can leave both doors open so we'll hear Pen if she needs us. Usually, though, she sleeps quite soundly."

"I know how to get to Montana."

Her abrupt response irritated him. Did she think he would try to seduce her? "Come now, Sydney, I'm talking about making plans, not making love."

She pressed her lips tightly together as she considered her decision, and he fought the urge to touch her. In her highly agitated state, any movement toward her would only upset her.

"All right, for a few minutes."

He hadn't realized how much he was hoping for

her agreement until she walked past him and he released his pent-up breath.

In his room, Sydney took the only chair, sitting ramrod straight, watching him warily. He sat on the edge of the bed closest to her and spread out the map.

"We have two days before we should be at the ranch. How much time do you have?" He didn't want to leave Sydney before he had to. To protect her, of course.

"I have to be in Denver by the evening of the next day."

He studied the map. "Hmmm, I figure it's about seven hundred and fifty to eight hundred miles to the ranch. And it looks like it's about that far from the ranch to Denver."

"Why don't you want to fly? You'd have more time with your family that way."

"Trying to get rid of us?"

She immediately shook her head. Her quick denial pleased him.

"I explained earlier."

"I could buy the tickets for you."

Her quiet offer displeased him. Of course she could. But that would mean leaving her behind. "We would still be recognized. No one knew we would be at that restaurant this evening, but those women still disturbed our meal."

"I realize now how difficult your travels have been. And why you're so angry with your mother."

"I'm glad you finally understand. It's okay. But that's why I've criticized my mother. You probably had a great mum.'' He hadn't delved much into her past, assuming she criticized his complaints about his mother because she loved hers—but she paled at his words.

''Sydney? What's wrong? Did I say something hurtful?''

She shook her head.

''Come on, darling, explain yourself.''

She looked away and he thought she was going to continue to stonewall him, but finally she said, ''My mother is still alive but we aren't close.''

Something in her voice made him want to question her more. ''Where is she?''

''She lives in New Jersey.''

''With you?''

''No. She lives in a nursing home for Alzheimer's patients. She wouldn't recognize me if I wore a name tag.'' Then, to his surprise, she added with a rueful smile, ''And if she did recognize me, she wouldn't be particularly happy to see me.''

''I'm sure you're wrong.'' He couldn't imagine anyone unhappy to see Sydney, especially her mother.

Sydney suddenly relaxed, chuckling. ''You sound like my father, always trying to convince me that Mother cared about me.''

''I don't understand.''

''My mother was always fragile. At least, that's how my dad explained it. She didn't want to deal with me. Every summer, I rode in the truck with my dad. I was desolate in the winter when he made trips without me.''

"Even when you were Pen's age?"

"Yes. He hired a woman to take care of me until I was four. Then I traveled with him, until I started school. Then just during the summers."

"Your mother...."

"Was always glad when we left. She said I made too much noise."

He wanted to reach out, hold her against him, assure her that her mother was the problem, not her. But he knew what holding her would result in, and it wouldn't be comfort.

"About five years ago, Dad had to admit she couldn't function on her own. Especially when he went out of town."

"So he put her in a nursing home?"

"Yes. A very nice one."

"And that's why you work two jobs? Why your fiancé abandoned you?"

"'Fraid so." She stiffened her shoulders and changed the subject. "It doesn't matter. Your family is expecting you Friday night?"

He was still thinking about her response and nodded with a frown.

"Any particular time Friday night?"

"Early would be better. It will give us more time to visit with my sister-in-law, Liz, before she goes into the hospital Monday morning."

"What's wrong with her?"

"Hmm? Oh, nothing. She's going to have my heir."

"Oh, I'd forgotten Penelope told me that."

"I'd forgotten, also. And you knew then that I was the duke, didn't you? How do you know about inheritance laws in England? Is that standard study in American schools?"

"No, but I'm an anglophile. I studied English literature, read everything I could get my hands on."

"Have you ever visited England?" he asked, studying her, wishing he could touch her hair, which glistened in the lamplight.

Sydney laughed. "No. I can't afford it. But traveling to England is top of my list for someday."

"Why don't you come back with us when we return? You could stay with us and we'd show you our country." When she started to object, he added, "It would be my treat. After all, you've shown us your country. Turnabout is fair play. Isn't that what you Yanks say?"

Though she smiled, she also shook her head. "I'd love it, but I can't take time off from either job."

Frustrated, he asked, "Isn't there someone who can help you? In England, the government—"

"There are cheaper places, but I promised Dad she'd have the best of care."

And she always kept her promises, thought Robert. Unlike Celia, his wife. That was another wonderful thing about Sydney.

The urge to lean over and kiss her filled him and he barely stopped himself. She seemed to realize his intent; standing and stepping away, she returned to the earlier subject. "So, is your brother's baby the reason you won't remarry?"

"It means I don't have to worry about producing a male heir."

"Your mother must not think so."

He grimaced. "True. Mother always looks for a fairy-tale ending. She believed Celia would come to love me in the end, also."

Sydney paced to the window, putting more distance between them. "I'm sorry. Is this child your brother's first?"

"No, he has a delightful four-year-old daughter named Stacy. Pen is eager to renew her acquaintanceship with her cousin."

With a brisk air, as if it were not almost ten o'clock at night, with the two of them in a bedroom, Sydney in a soft robe and gown that outlined her figure, she came toward him. "Then we need to get her there as quickly as possible. I think I can have you there tomorrow evening if we get a very early start in the morning."

"Drive eight hundred miles in one day? That's ridiculous." And not what he'd planned.

"I'm willing."

"I'm not. I'd hoped we could drive maybe five hundred tomorrow and then take a side trip to Yellowstone Park in Wyoming. I've heard it's impressive."

"Even if we had time, they wouldn't let my truck in, Robert. The park's jam-packed every summer.

After the baby is born, maybe your brother will take you."

He stood and moved to her side. "Why do I get the impression you're eager to get rid of us?"

"You're being silly. But we both have deadlines, schedules we have to keep. We'll split up the miles equally, and have you at the ranch by four o'clock Friday."

He ducked his head to hide his grin. Any sign that he was pleased would have her scurrying for cover. "So, where shall we spend the night?"

"I'm not sure. I think we should take the back roads if they don't slow us down too much. There's less chance of being spotted that way."

"Good. And we can see more of America."

"Fine. Everything's decided. We'll have breakfast at eight and be on our way." Without waiting for his agreement, she hurried toward the door as if being chased.

Maybe she was. He knew he had only to touch her once to make her disappear into the other bedroom. Catching her arm, he pulled her to face him.

"Are you afraid of me?"

"Of course not."

"Then may I kiss you good-night?"

She stiffened. "Why?"

"Because I can't seem to think of anything else. I've wanted to kiss you again since we awoke this morning."

His honesty didn't seem to score him any points.

"Kissing wouldn't be wise. We both know...

whatever happens when we touch each other has nothing to do with our situations.''

''What situations?''

''We don't trust the opposite sex, remember? And neither of us is looking for a—a relationship.''

''I'm not looking for marriage. But I wouldn't mind—''

''No! I'm not willing to be your entertainment. I only offered a ride in my truck, nothing else.''

He grinned. ''I'm not talking about a sacrifice, Sydney. It seemed to me you enjoyed our kiss this morning, too.''

''Yes, I did.''

Her honesty pleased him.

Until she continued. ''But I don't think—''

Without waiting for her to finish, he swept her into his arms and lowered his lips to hers.

If anything, the anticipation he'd been experiencing all day made her touch even more pleasurable. Her soft lips melded to his and she opened to him at once. His hands stroked her lithe body, holding it tightly against him.

He might have thought the groan he heard came from her lips if he hadn't lifted his mouth briefly, seeking an even deeper taking of her kiss.

''What was that?'' she gasped, pushing away from him.

''Probably someone else,'' he whispered and reached for her again.

A whimper of pain jerked them both to attention.

As if one, they came to the same realization.

''Penelope!''

Chapter Nine

"Pen, what's wrong?" Robert sat on the side of the bed.

"Sweetie, are you sick?" Sydney knelt down next to him.

Penelope slowly opened her eyes. "My tummy hurts, Daddy."

He stroked Penelope's forehead to determine whether the child was running a fever. Turning to Sydney, he shook his head. "Is it a sharp pain or a dull ache?" he asked.

"I don't know. It hurts!" Penelope cried.

"Do you know of a hospital around here?" Robert asked, his face reflecting his panic.

"In a moment. Penny, will you let me listen to your tummy?"

"Why? Is it going to talk to you?" The child appeared momentarily distracted by Sydney's question.

"Not exactly, but sometimes when you've eaten something that upsets your tummy, it growls." With a smile, Sydney lifted Penny's pajama top and placed her ear against the warm skin.

When she lifted her head, frowning, she discovered Robert and Penelope staring at her, waiting for a pronouncement.

With a shrug of her shoulders, she said, "I can't hear anything. When did it start to hurt?"

"It hurt this afternoon, but I didn't say anything because Dad said not to bother you."

"Oh, Pen." Robert cuddled his daughter against him. "I didn't mean if you were sick. I had no idea—" He broke off, anguish on his face.

"Of course, you didn't," Sydney reassured him. Robert was a sexy man, she thought, but he was at his most attractive when he cared for his child.

"What do we do now?" Robert asked.

"Go ask Mrs. Wright if she has a hot water bottle. Sometimes heat will make a tummy feel better."

An hour later, after numerous consultations among the three adults, Robert decided they should take Penelope to the emergency room at the local hospital.

"I still think you should give her my medicine," Mrs. Wright offered again. She'd been trying to convince Robert to give the child some over-the-counter indigestion cures.

"Thank you, Mrs. Wright," Sydney said, "but I don't think Penny's stomachache is caused by something she ate."

Sydney didn't want to tell Robert what she thought the problem was. She'd had a similar stomachache when she was nine and driving with her dad. It had turned out to be appendicitis.

"I think we'll see a doctor just to be on the safe

side, Mrs. Wright. But we appreciate your assistance," Robert said smoothly. "Where is the nearest hospital?"

While Mrs. Wright gave him directions, Sydney gathered up some clothes and slipped across the hall to change.

When she came out, Robert had wrapped Penelope in a lightweight blanket.

"Oh, there you are," Robert exclaimed, as if he'd lost her. "Are you ready?"

"Yes. How are you doing, Penny?"

"It hurts," the child moaned, clinging to her father.

"We'll have you to the hospital in no time." She looked at Robert. "You have the directions?"

"Yes."

They reached the hospital only a few minutes later, Robert carrying Penelope in his arms. They were told by a busy nurse to sit and wait. For the first time, Sydney saw Robert pull rank when he realized his daughter would not be seen immediately.

"I'm the Duke of Hereford. I insist my child see a doctor at once."

The nurse at the receiving desk immediately called someone, and several minutes later a doctor introduced himself.

"My lord, I'm Dr. Charles Lindale. How may I help you?"

"My child, Lady Penelope, is experiencing stomach pains, for no apparent reason. I want her examined at once."

After a quick conference with the nurse, the doctor led the way to one of their cubicles. Robert lay Penelope down on the examining table.

"Would you care to wait in my office?" the doctor asked.

Sydney almost rolled her eyes. She'd been in a number of emergency rooms, but she'd never been invited to wait in a doctor's office rather than with the crowds in the waiting room.

Robert appeared unimpressed. "No, thank you. We'll stay here with Penelope."

Sydney saw relief fill the child's face. Taking her hand, Sydney smiled at her and leaned down to whisper, "I think he's used to getting his way."

Penelope giggled and then gasped as the movement brought more pain.

The doctor immediately began questioning her about what she was feeling as the nurse took a blood sample, quickly, before Penelope could become fearful. The doctor felt her stomach, then excused himself.

"I think I owe you an apology," Sydney said to Penelope, trying to take her mind off her ills.

"What for?"

"I didn't remember I should call you 'Lady Penelope.'" She looked at Robert. "Or your father, 'my lord.'"

The little girl smiled and squeezed Sydney's hand. "It's okay. Our family doesn't use titles, and you're almost like family. Isn't she, Dad?"

Sydney shuddered as Robert's arm came around

her, then quickly composed herself, hoping he hadn't noticed.

"Of course she is, Pen."

"Besides, it would give away Dad's secret if you called him 'my lord.'"

"I don't think his identity is a secret anymore," Sydney reminded the child.

The doctor returned with another man in a white coat. "My lord, may I present Dr. Albert Crowder, a distinguished surgeon?"

"Why are you introducing a surgeon?"

"My diagnosis is appendicitis. Dr. Crowder is needed to confirm it. Then he will perform the surgery. If you agree," the doctor hastily added.

Again Robert tightened his hold on Sydney. With his other hand, he reached out and stroked Penelope's forehead. "I see."

"With your permission, my lord?" Dr. Crowder asked. However, he didn't really wait for Robert to agree. Instead, he addressed Penelope. "How are you, my lady? I understand your tummy isn't well."

"No," Penelope agreed in a small voice. "What's an appendi—what you said?"

"Ah. It's when the appendix in your tummy gets sick and we have to remove it."

"Will it hurt?"

"Of course not. We'll put you to sleep and when you wake up, everything will be taken care of. You rest a lot for the next few days, eat lots of ice cream, and it will never bother you again."

"Ice cream?" Penelope repeated. "See, Dad? If

I'd finished my ice cream, I wouldn't have gotten sick.''

"That's not what the doctor meant, Pen, but we'll see that you get lots of ice cream afterwards.''

While they talked, the doctor was feeling around on Penelope's stomach. Then he nodded to Dr. Lindale before looking at Robert again. "I confirm the diagnosis, my lord. If you have someone you wish to have perform the surgery, we could try to delay it until his arrival, but I don't recommend doing so. There is always the potential for the appendix to rupture.''

Robert frowned, then looked at Sydney. "What do you think, Sydney? Shall we let them go ahead?''

For the first time, both doctors looked at Sydney, seemingly surprised that Robert would consult her.

"I apologize, my lady. I didn't realize you were Lady Penelope's mother,'' Dr. Crowder said. "My associate told me Lord Hereford was unmarried.''

"I'm a friend, Doctor. Robert, I think you should let Dr. Crowder go ahead and operate. It's not a complicated surgery and I'm sure they'll take good care of Penelope.''

"Will you stay with me?'' Penelope asked her, clinging to her hand.

"Your dad and I can't go into surgery with you, sweetie, because we might have germs. But we'll be waiting for you. When you wake up, we'll be beside your bed.''

"Promise? Promise, Dad?''

"Of course, love." He bent over and kissed his daughter's forehead. "Right, doctors?"

Sydney thought his question was more of a command, and both doctors hurriedly promised him and his child.

Almost at once, there was a flurry of activity. Robert was escorted out to sign papers allowing the procedure, and several nurses prepped Penelope for surgery. Sydney was permitted to remain beside the little girl, holding her hand, until the anesthetic took hold.

"She's under. You can release her hand," the nurse suggested. "We need to take her to surgery."

Sydney found it difficult to let go. She wanted to protest, to insist on accompanying Penny, but she knew she was being ridiculous. She did make one request, however. "Her father will want to see her before you take her away."

"Lord Hereford? He's coming now. Handsome man," the nurse added, watching Sydney. "You two are—?"

"Yes, we are," Robert's deep voice assured the nurse before she could finish her question.

Sydney's startled gaze fell on him as he walked into the cubicle, then quickly looked away. "They're ready to take Penelope, uh, Lady Penelope upstairs."

"Yes," Robert agreed with a sigh as he stared down at his only child. He leaned over and kissed her forehead again. Then, after stroking her cheek, he stepped back, holding out a hand for Sydney. She never even thought of refusing his unspoken request.

They stood against the wall as the bed was wheeled out. "She looks so small," Robert muttered.

Dr. Lindale stepped in. "If you two would like to wait in the doctors' lounge, someone will let you know as soon as you can see your daughter. And you won't be disturbed there."

"Thank you, we'd like that," Robert said and turned to follow the doctor, pulling Sydney along behind him.

ROBERT SAT ON THE SOFA several hours later, Sydney's sleeping form in his arms, waiting for word that Penelope had been moved to the recovery room.

A nurse had already called from the operating room to let him know that the operation had been a success, and relief had filled him at those words. He'd never suffered a longer night, knowing that his child was at risk.

Sydney had been a terrific support. She'd finally collapsed after that call, relaxing against him, and soon sleeping deeply. Considering the day she'd had, he was surprised she'd held out as long as she had.

Her concern for Pen had been motherly, whether Sydney realized it or not. He knew Pen's own mother, Celia, had she been alive, wouldn't have altered her schedule one iota to see about her child. Sydney, however, had suffered to remain at Penelope's side.

He supposed he should be grateful to his mother for her chicanery or he might never have met Sydney. He could've sworn he'd never trust a woman again, but Sydney was different. If nothing else, he knew she loved Penelope.

She shifted against him, heightening his awareness of her warm body. Perhaps he should reconsider his intention to never marry. Penelope would be better with a mother to attend to her needs.

And he had a few needs Sydney could attend to, also.

The idea took hold, much to his surprise. He'd only known the woman three days, but they had been intensive days and nights. Never once had Sydney tried to use him for her advantage.

In fact, he'd presented her with several opportunities to force him into marriage. Sydney had even thought it was her fault when they'd woken up in bed in each other's arms.

And when he'd told Carl they were engaged, she'd chastised him, knowing even then that he was the duke supposedly looking for a wife.

Maybe she didn't like him.

That idea pained him. Then he dismissed it. It wasn't that he was irresistible. No, it was that Sydney, until she remembered who he was, had never resisted. Like now. She cuddled against him with all the trust of a wife.

The phone rang and he eased Sydney aside to answer it.

"Your daughter is going into Recovery on the third floor. The nurse will let you sit with her until she awakens, if you like."

"Thank you. We'll be there at once."

He hung up the phone to find Sydney watching him, her blue eyes wide with concern.

"Pen's in Recovery. We can go there and see her."

"Oh, wonderful," Sydney responded, relief filling her voice. "I'm sorry I fell asleep."

"Don't worry. You were due a little rest. Let's go see our—Penelope. We promised we would be there when she awoke."

He'd almost made a mistake. The time would come to speak to Sydney of their future, but now was not it. He had to concern himself with Penelope's recovery.

Sydney, of course, would accept. The life of a duchess was certainly preferable to that of a truck driver.

All he had to concern himself with was his mother's reaction. She wanted him married again, but he suspected she had in mind someone well established in society.

Unlike Sydney.

PENELOPE FROWNED. Why couldn't she open her eyes? With great effort, she finally managed to do so, then closed them immediately. The light hurt.

"Penny? Are you awake, sweetie?"

"Pen? How are you feeling?"

The two voices reassured Penelope that all was right in her world. Mummy and Dad were there.

She'd almost drifted off again when she remembered she didn't have a mummy. Oh, yes. Sydney.

"Dad, Sydney," she whispered, a smile forming, then she subsided into sleep again.

The next time she stirred, she opened her eyes more easily. "Dad? Where are you? Sydney?"

She'd scarcely finished calling when the two of them were hovering over her bed. She tried to lick her lips, but her tongue felt swollen.

"Are you thirsty, Penny?" Sydney asked. "How about some ice chips?"

She nodded.

"You've had a good long sleep, poppet. Are you feeling rested?" her father asked.

She shook her head, then stopped. That didn't feel good. "When do I get ice cream?"

Sydney, having come back into her line of vision with the ice chips, chuckled. "Not yet, little one. First you have to eat ice chips."

It occurred to Penelope that being in hospital wasn't all bad. Having her two favorite people beside her was neat. But it also struck her that Sydney might not be around much longer.

"Sydney?"

"Yes, Penny?"

"You're not going to leave now, are you? I didn't intend to come to the hospital. You won't go away, will you?"

Sydney smoothed her forehead. "Don't make wrinkles, sweetie. I'm not going to leave. Besides, you'll be out of here in no time."

"And you'll be able to travel in Sydney's bed. It will be perfect," her father added.

"What about when we get to Uncle Pete's?"

Her father took her hand. "You'll be able to see everyone. But you and Stacy won't be able to run around like you usually do. Okay?"

She squeezed her father's hand. "No, Dad, that's not what I meant. What about Sydney?"

Her father said nothing, only cleared his throat.

She twisted with a painful grimace until she could see Sydney.

"Penelope, you know I have to go on to Denver. I've already told you I have a job to do."

"Can't you stay for just a little while?"

"I'll stay overnight, so you'll have time to show me everything. Okay?"

No, it wasn't okay. But all she could do right now was agree. She nodded, then said, "I'm tired," and closed her eyes.

She tried to stay awake long enough to devise a plan. Because she didn't intend to return to England without Sydney. She was the perfect mum, and Penelope had to convince her dad that she would be the perfect wife, too.

Maybe Nana would help.

SEVERAL HOURS LATER, Penelope, still groggy, was transferred into a regular room. Once she was tucked in, Robert insisted Sydney relax on the couch. Though she protested, her eyes closed immediately and her breathing deepened.

Robert waited until both females were sleeping deeply. Then he reached for the phone to make the call he'd been dreading. The phone was answered by his brother's longtime housekeeper.

"Maisie? This is Robert. Is my mother awake?"

"Why, a'course she is. Mary Margaret, it's Robert."

There was a rustling sound before the Dowager Duchess of Hereford spoke. "Robert, where are you? I've been so worried. It was almost as if you disappeared off the face of the earth."

"I'm in a hospital."

"A hospital? Are you hurt?"

"Pen had her appendix removed."

"Oh, my poor baby. Let me talk to her."

"Mother, she's just out of surgery and still sleeping. But I can assure you she is fine."

"I'll be on the first plane. What is the name of the hospital?"

"Your coming is not necessary, Mother. I only called because it's possible that we may not arrive exactly when we planned."

"Of course it is necessary for me to come. You are a man. Penelope needs the feminine touch. It is so sad that the child has no mother."

Robert gritted his teeth. "Mother, you have caused me a great deal of difficulty with your scheme to marry me off. I won't allow your interference again."

"I only want to be there for Penelope since she has no mother."

"She has Sydney, so don't—"

"Who is Sydney? Some strange man is not going to minister to my granddaughter!"

"Sydney is not a man, and she's not a stranger!" Robert ripped back. Penelope stirred, reminding Robert he needed to keep his voice low.

"Sydney is a woman?" his mother asked, interest rising in her voice.

"Yes." He said nothing else. He hadn't meant to mention Sydney at this point, but somehow with his mother he always lost control.

"Is she coming with you to the ranch?"

"Yes."

"Are you sure Penelope is all right?"

"Quite sure, Mother."

"Then let us know when you'll arrive. And give Penelope my love."

To his surprise, his mother hung up before he could say anything else. Not that he knew what to say. But it was strange that his mother had not asked a billion questions about Sydney.

Very strange indeed.

LADY HEREFORD HUNG UP the phone, a pleased smile on her lips.

"What's wrong?" Pete asked as he stood up to go to the barn. "Robert and Pen okay?"

"Penelope had her appendix removed. She's fine…and Robert's found a woman!"

Pete exchanged a look with his very pregnant wife, Liz. Then he turned back. "Mother, you promised there'd be no more interfering. I suspect you've

caused Robert a lot of problems with your announcement to the papers and your appearance on television."

"I only told the papers he was considering remar-
riage, and I can't help it if Oprah was interested."
She did her best to sound abused, hoping to get a
little sympathy from her frowning son. "Besides,
you wouldn't have found Liz without my interference."

Pete shook his head at the hopelessness of making
his mother understand. Then he kissed Liz goodbye,
warning her to rest, said goodbye to Maisie and his
mother, and departed.

"Now, what are you not tellin' us?" Maisie said
as soon as the door closed.

"Her name is Sydney. Robert didn't intend to tell
me, I'm sure, but when I said Pen needed a woman
around, he insisted Sydney would take care of her."

"Do you know how old Sydney is? She could be
grandmotherly, you know," Liz said.

"No, he wouldn't be defensive about a grandmother. I'm sure she's young and attractive." The
dowager stared into space, as if she could visualize
the woman. "And he's bringing her to the ranch."

"Mary Margaret," Maisie began informally, having lived on the ranch since the dowager was a little
girl, "you heard Pete. He'll be unhappy with you if
you interfere."

"I would never do that," she replied with a big
smile. "But a little encouragement can't hurt."

Chapter Ten

The hospital decided to post security guards outside Penelope's room because of the number of inquiries they received after the news broke about the duke's arrival.

With such reinforcements, the threesome inside the room were undisturbed. Robert insisted that both Penelope and Sydney sleep.

"Robert, is everything all right?" Sydney whispered a few hours later.

Robert put down the paper and turned to her. "Everything's fine. They had Pen out of bed and walking before they fed her lunch. She's supposed to take another turn after her nap. Then, if all goes well, she'll be released tomorrow morning, and we'll be on our way."

"We can leave tomorrow morning?" Sydney repeated with relief.

"Yes. Amazing, isn't it?"

"Yes, it is. If we drive all day tomorrow, we'll get to the ranch late tomorrow night, and still be on schedule."

Of course, she wouldn't get to spend any time with them on the ranch or see the horses as Penelope had planned, but that couldn't be helped. She had a job to do.

Again, as she thought of their time together coming to an end, sadness filled her. So much had happened in the past few days that she felt as if she were a different person. Without Robert and Penelope, her life would be dull and repetitive.

"I think you should call whoever is in charge and tell them you can't be there on Sunday."

Sydney had been lost in her thoughts and didn't hear all of Robert's statement. When he repeated himself, she stared in horror. "I can't do that, Robert. I promised."

"We didn't know Pen would get sick. Just explain that you'll be delayed a few days."

"Robert, I promised. Roy won't give me the plum jobs if I don't keep my schedule." He might not give her any jobs at all. And then what would she do?

"Sydney, you can't possibly drive until late tomorrow night and then get up and make it to Denver the next day. I'll make up the amount you might lose."

She didn't want to take his money. She wasn't like the rest of the American women chasing him, thinking only of lining their pockets. Already, after telling him about her mother's nursing home, she feared he would think she was trying to trap him.

"I can't."

Almost before her eyes Robert changed into the

autocratic duke. "Call whoever is in charge and ask."

"No."

"I will not accept that answer. The least you can do is call. Or give me the number and I'll call." His handsome face was stern and unrelenting.

An hysterical giggle bubbled up inside her. She could just hear a conversation between Roy and the Duke of Hereford. That would never do. "I'll call, but if Roy needs me to be there, I'm going. No matter what you say."

Robert stood by her side as she placed a call to Roy, the scheduler.

"Roy, it's Sydney. I have a problem and wondered if I could delay the pickup in Denver until…Monday." She shot a quick glance at Robert. Had he meant for her to stay at the ranch an extra day?

"Longer," he murmured, an arm slipping around her.

How tempted she was to lean against his hard frame, to draw from his strength, to let him dominate her. But she couldn't. Such behavior would make her weak. She needed to be strong.

"If you can't—" she began when Roy said nothing.

"What's the problem?" Roy demanded in his gravelly voice.

"A friend had an appendectomy and—"

"The duke?"

She should've known Roy would have heard the

rumors. He was in contact with most of the drivers. "No, his child. I hate to leave until she's a little more recovered."

"I can work it out if you're sure you'll be there Monday morning at eight. But don't get too involved with these people, Syd. They're not your kind, you know?"

"Thanks, Roy," she said, ignoring his advice. After all, she'd already told herself the same thing.

"Eight o'clock, Monday. If you don't come through, I won't be able to schedule you anymore. Got it?"

"Yes, Roy, and I'll be there. Thanks." She hung up the phone and turned to face Robert. "He'll give me until Monday morning."

"You'll be too tired. You should've asked for a week," Robert insisted.

She drew in a deep breath. "You seem to forget that I need to earn a living, Robert. Even if he'd give me a week, I can't afford to take a vacation."

"I said I would pay—"

"No! I don't want your money."

He caught her shoulders and Sydney feared he would pull her against him again. She longed for him to do so, but she also knew she should not.

"Sydney, I have plenty of money. I don't understand—"

Wrenching her shoulders from his hold, she backed against the wall. "I don't need your money."

"Why won't you take any assistance? Money

doesn't matter to me, and I don't want it to matter to you, either.''

''It's personal.''

He stared at her in surprise. ''Everything between us is personal. Isn't it?''

She couldn't deny the truth in those words. But she was reluctant to let him into her life. It would leave too big a hole when he left. ''Roy won't schedule me anymore if I'm not there on Monday. While I appreciate your offer, I have to think about the future.''

His gaze softened and he reached out to stroke her cheek. ''You're driving yourself too hard.''

''Don't make me out to be a saint. I choose to keep my promise to my father. So it's up to me to do the work.''

He said nothing more but did what she'd dreaded—yet longed for. Wrapping his arms around her, he cradled her against him. Sydney didn't ever want to leave the wonderful sanctuary of his embrace.

But she had to.

Pulling back, she said, ''I think it's your turn on the sofa. You should nap while Penny is sleeping. I'll take care of her if she wakes.''

''I know you will,'' he said, smiling tenderly at her. ''But I'm all right. I don't need much sleep.''

''I may need you to do some driving for me,'' she said, lying. ''So you need as much sleep as me.''

His shoulders slumped and he gave her a half

smile. "All right, you've made your point. But you'll wake me if anything goes wrong?"

"I promise."

His lips grazed hers, then were gone before she could even think of responding. Then he settled onto the sofa, the pillow tucked beneath his cheek. Sydney covered him with the blanket and he was asleep almost before she finished.

She stood staring down at him, wondering how she would ever forget him.

"I THINK I COULD get very spoilt if I hung out with you and your dad for much longer," Sydney told Penelope. The two were pigging out on ice cream she'd requested earlier. And since the request came from the Duke of Hereford's party, it was delivered at once.

"What do you mean?" the child asked.

"Whenever your father wants something, he only has to ask for it. People rush to meet his every demand."

Penelope frowned at her. "Isn't that good?"

"Yes, sweetheart, it's very good, but it's not real life."

"Why?"

"Because most people don't have the power or money to inspire such service."

"Nana says we mustn't ask for too much," Penelope confessed, "but I asked for a pony last Christmas and I got one."

"Do you have a place to keep a pony?"

"Oh, yes, Sydney," Penelope said, chuckling. "What a funny question."

"Why is it a funny question?"

"Because we have lots of room. Dad has big horses, lots of them, but I wanted one my size. My cousin has a pony and she's younger than me."

"But she lives on a ranch."

"Yes, but our estate is almost as big."

Sydney realized she still didn't comprehend the differences between her life and Penelope's. But she was beginning to. "Do you go to school?"

"Yes, Angus takes me every morning."

"Who is Angus?"

"Our chauffeur. Sometimes Dad drives me, but often he has to work."

"I see. Well, I think—"

The phone rang and she snatched it up, hoping the noise wouldn't rouse Robert.

"Hello?"

"I would like to speak to either Lady Penelope or Lord Hereford, please." The female voice was autocratic, reminding Sydney of Robert when he was acting the role of duke.

"I'm sorry, they're not available for telephone calls." Sydney was sure Robert wouldn't take calls from strangers.

"Listen to me, young lady. I have already dealt with the telephone operator. I will not tolerate any interference from you. I insist on speaking to my granddaughter or son at once."

Sydney froze. The Dowager Duchess of Hereford?

She covered the receiver with her hand. "This lady says she's your grandmother."

"Nana? Let me talk to her," Penelope sounded as autocratic as her father. Surely it was in the blood.

PENELOPE WAS THRILLED that she was being given an opportunity to talk to Nana. Together they could come up with a plan. But she had to get Sydney out of the way.

"Uh, Sydney, could you go get me some more ice cream while I talk to Nana. It makes me feel so much better."

"I haven't finished mine, Pen. You can have it."

"Oh, no. I couldn't take yours. Will you please ask the nurse?"

Sydney smiled and nodded, then left the room.

"Nana?"

"What is going on, child? How are you?"

"I'm fine," Penelope said briskly. "But we must hurry. I've found the perfect mummy."

"Sydney?"

"You know about her?" Penelope asked in surprise.

"I talked with your father earlier and he mentioned the young woman. Why do you think she's the perfect mummy?"

"She loves me. And I know she likes Dad. And she's very pretty."

"How nice. Who are her people?"

"Her people?"

"Her family. Where does she live?"

"She lives in a truck, Nana. It's neat." Silence greeted her words. "Nana?"

"Yes, dear. Does your father think she's perfect?"

"I think so. He said she's lots prettier than the lady who was going to take her clothes off."

Her grandmother gasped. "Child, what is going on there?"

"Lots of ladies want to marry Dad. But I want Sydney. Will you help me, Nana?"

"I'm doing the best I can, child. You say she lives in a truck?"

"Yes. I'm going to ride on her bed after my operation. And I saw you on the telly!"

"Did your father?"

"Yes, and he wasn't very happy."

"Oh, dear, I'd hoped— No wonder he was so abrupt. Well, I will certainly see about helping you, child. This Sydney is coming to the ranch, isn't she?"

"Yes, but she says she has to go back to work. I don't want her to."

"Well, together we'll think of something. You take good care of yourself, my love. Promise?"

"I promise. Do you want to talk to Dad? He's sleeping."

"No. I'll be waiting for you. Drive carefully."

"We will. Oh, Sydney's back. Do you want to talk to her?"

Sydney froze in the doorway, holding Penelope's ice cream. Why couldn't she have taken a few minutes longer?

"Nana wants to talk to you," Penelope said, holding out the phone.

In a panic Sydney turned to Robert, but he was sleeping soundly. Reluctantly, she took the receiver. "Hello?"

"Sydney? This is Lady Hereford, Robert's mother. I wanted to express my appreciation for your assistance to my son and granddaughter."

Relaxing slightly, Sydney murmured, "You're welcome. But really I haven't done that much."

"I suspect you're being modest. I understand you're coming to the ranch with them?"

"Um, I'm driving them there."

"Oh? What kind of vehicle are you driving?"

Sydney swallowed. "A truck."

Silence followed and she couldn't help imagining the dowager duchess on the floor in a dead faint.

Instead, the brisk voice said, "How nice. Where are you from? Who is your family?"

"My lady, I'm just driving them," Sydney said desperately, hoping to dispel the notion that she was part of their circle.

"Yes, of course, dear, but surely you don't mind a little conversation. After all, I like to know with whom my granddaughter is associating."

Sydney stiffened. "My family is from New Jersey. And you would never have heard of them. I'll be glad to drive Robert...I mean, Lord Hereford and Lady Penelope to the nearest airport, if that is what he prefers. That way Penny...Lady Penelope won't be associating with me any longer than necessary."

"Dear child, I didn't mean to insult you. I'm sure you're proper company for my darling granddaughter. She seems to appreciate you very much. As I'm sure Robert does."

The emptiness that followed begged Sydney to tell the woman about Robert's relationship with her, but Sydney pressed her lips together and waited.

The lady sighed. "Is Robert still sleeping?"

"Yes, my lady."

"Robert never takes naps. Is he all right?"

"We got very little sleep last night because of Lady Penelope's surgery."

"Oh, of course. Well, perhaps I should speak with Pen again."

"Of course," Sydney agreed, glad to end their awkward exchange. She handed the phone to Penelope and sat down again.

"Nana, Sydney got me more ice cream," Penelope announced at once, as if that news was more important than anything else.

After a pause, the child said, "No, I like it. It has a big bed in it."

Sydney could just imagine what the dowager duchess thought about that information. She didn't have long to wait.

"Yes, me and Dad and Sydney slept in it. It was very comfortable." Penelope beamed at Sydney.

"Penny—" Sydney began and then subsided against the chair. What difference did it make? She was sure the dowager duchess had already made up her mind about the stranger driving her family.

A family she'd never see again after she got them to the ranch.

"Jeans."

Sydney's gaze snapped back to Penelope's face. What question prompted that response? Sydney looked down at her jeans-clad legs. It certainly summed up her wardrobe.

And she supposed it told Lady Hereford, if she was in any doubt, that Sydney wasn't of their class.

She closed her eyes, wishing she didn't have to listen to any more of this one-sided conversation.

"Pen, who are you talking to?" Robert suddenly demanded, rising from the sofa and reaching for the telephone.

Sydney wasn't sure whether Robert's intervention was a blessing or a disaster.

Chapter Eleven

Somehow Robert wasn't surprised that it was his mother.

"How are you, dear boy?"

"Fine, Mother. Why are you calling?"

"I wanted to see how Pen was doing, of course."

"She's fine." He feared Sydney would think he was being rude to his mother—something that seemed to bother her—but he knew his mother. She wouldn't settle for hearing about Pen's health.

"I talked to Sydney, also. She has a lovely voice. Pen said she's as pretty as she sounds."

"She's fine."

"Pen also mentioned you shared a bed with her."

Robert glared at Penelope, then regretted his action. Both Sydney and Penelope stared at him in surprise. "Our sleeping arrangements are none of your business, Mother."

Sydney turned pale.

"I only asked out of concern. I want you to get married again, but only to the right woman."

"I don't think that topic has come up, Mother."

"But surely you don't want to set a bad example for Penelope. She wouldn't understand."

He pressed his lips in frustration. It wasn't that he couldn't answer his mother. But he couldn't answer in front of the two pair of ears carefully listening to his side of the conversation.

"I'll explain everything when we arrive, Mother."

"Of course, dear. And I'll meet Sydney. Will she be staying long?"

He noticed Sydney's anxious look. It was tempting to tell his mother of plans that were growing in his head—plans to keep Sydney with him always—but he hadn't discussed that with Sydney, yet.

Finally, he settled for an indefinite "I don't know."

"Of course, we have plenty of room. Enough for each of you to have a separate bedroom, even though Liz's mother lives here now, too."

"Good."

"Robert, you're not revealing much," she returned, frustration in her voice.

"No, I'm not. I have to go now. It's time for Penelope to walk."

"Already? But the surgery was just this morning."

"She walked mid-morning. They believe in getting surgical patients out of bed quickly these days."

"Well, give her my love, and we'll look forward to seeing you tomorrow evening."

"No, probably Saturday evening. We don't want to drive too far Pen's first day out of the hospital."

"Very well. Be careful."

"We will." He hung up the phone with a sigh of relief. Having a conversation with his mother, especially lately, was like running an obstacle course.

"My mother appreciates your kindness to us," he said to Sydney.

She wiped the anxious expression from her face. "She expressed her thanks to me." Without looking at him, she began stacking the dishes. "If you'll open the door, I'll take this tray back to the nurses' station."

"Why not ask them to come get it?"

"Because we've caused a great deal of extra work already. It's the least I can do."

He moved over to the door, but paused as she came up behind him. "Why do I think you're trying to get away from me?" he whispered.

She raised her chin, but didn't look at him. "I'm trying to be helpful."

"Did my mother upset you?"

"Open the door, Robert. My arms are getting tired."

As an attempt to avoid talking to him, her complaint wasn't a good one. He knew just how strong her arms were. "My mother's opinion isn't important, Sydney. She doesn't know you."

She stubbornly kept her chin down, waiting.

In frustration, Robert snapped open the lock and held the door for her. "We'll continue this discussion later," he said as she walked past him.

She didn't look back.

SYDNEY HAD NO INTENTION of continuing the discussion later. It was obvious what his mother thought. Her mention of sleeping arrangements to Robert showed that she thought Sydney and Robert were already involved.

Well, they were, but not *that* involved. And Sydney had no intention of letting things go that far. She already knew how desolate her life would seem when Robert and Penelope were gone. She didn't need the added physical craving that making love with him would create.

The difficulty was keeping her distance from Robert, who seemed to think casual touches, even kisses, were acceptable. Nothing about them felt casual to Sydney.

"SYDNEY, WE WAITED for you to come back before I walked. I wanted you to see," Penelope assured her. Scooting to the edge of the bed, she held out her arms to her father. "Come on, Dad. Let's show Sydney."

"All right, poppet. Don't move too quickly." He eased his daughter down until her feet rested on the floor. "She's supposed to walk for ten or fifteen minutes. We have a limited itinerary since we must remain in the room, but Pen doesn't mind."

He escorted his daughter around the room while keeping a close eye on Sydney. After a few minutes, she offered to take over, and he sat back in the straight chair by the bed, watching the two females in his life walk back and forth.

If nothing else, he was assured of Penelope's feelings about Sydney as they walked about the room. The child stared up at her with adoring eyes. Sydney teased her, bringing chuckles to her lips.

When Penelope launched into tales about her past, Sydney listened with patience, giving Pen her entire attention.

What a contrast to the women who had pursued him. Not just the hysterical females of the past few days, but those in England, also. Once Celia died, making him eligible again, he found himself hemmed in by women wanting him either for themselves, or for their daughters.

Occasionally one would realize how important Pen was to him and would approach him through his daughter. But if he showed even a flicker of interest, the woman would immediately abandon Pen to her fate and concentrate on Robert.

More and more he'd withdrawn from all contact with women, trying to protect both himself and Pen. His mother, in contrast, had grown more and more desperate to find a wife for him—resulting in her announcement to the papers.

Robert chuckled as he studied Sydney. With her long braid, jeans and T-shirt, she might appear to be the last woman his mother would want him to marry.

But the wisps of russet hair framed a beautiful face, and the tight jeans and T-shirt caressed a tempting, womanly figure. Most important of all, they covered a pure heart and a gentle spirit.

He had vowed never to trust a woman again, but

he could do nothing but trust Sydney. Trust her, not *love* her, he hurriedly assured himself. He wasn't going to offer his heart to anyone ever again. But he could trust her.

And he desired her.

Oh, yes. Just watching her was becoming difficult, as he imagined touching every part of her anatomy. Since he'd avoided women, he'd also avoided intimacy for too long. At the prospect of loving Sydney, his body was stirring, with a hunger almost too powerful to control.

"Robert, what are you thinking about?" Sydney asked sharply, drawing him from his thoughts.

"Uh, about how well the two of you are doing with Pen's exercises. Are you tired, poppet? Time to go back to bed?" he asked, standing, hoping to distract Sydney before she could ask any more questions.

"Yes, I'm tired. I think I need more ice cream," Penelope said, shooting looks at both him and Sydney.

Sydney remained silent, but Robert was determined to involve her in decisions about Penelope. "What do you think, Sydney? Shall we ask for more ice cream?"

"No, I think not," Sydney said calmly, not wavering even when Penelope sent her an incredulous glare. "It's too close to dinner. Perhaps you could have ice cream for dessert if you eat well."

"Good idea," Robert agreed.

"But, Dad, that's not fair. I did my exercises!" Penelope protested, still looking angry.

"The exercises are for your own good, Pen, not to earn more ice cream."

"Nana would've let me have it," Penelope said with a pout. "I'm going to tell her you were both mean to me."

Robert watched Sydney closely, wondering how she would react to Penelope's threat. After all, though he had experience being a parent, she had not.

She smiled at the little girl, tucked the blanket under her and kissed her cheek. "Okay."

Penelope frowned at her, but Robert wasn't willing to be so accepting. "I think you owe Sydney an apology, poppet. She was trying to do what was best for you."

"But I want ice cream," Penelope insisted, crossing her arms over her little body.

"And you think ice cream is more important than Sydney's feelings?" Robert asked softly.

He knew he'd reached Pen because her eyes teared up.

"I'm sorry, Sydney. I didn't mean to hurt your feelings," she said and sniffed, wiping a tear away.

"Of course you didn't, sweetheart," Sydney reassured her, giving her a hug. "You're just tired from all that excellent exercising. You want to watch television now?"

Penelope was distracted from her behavior, but she remembered to offer her father an apology, too, before the cartoons she loved took over completely.

Robert led Sydney to the sofa and pulled the straight-back chair over to its side. "You'll make an excellent parent," he assured her as he sat down beside her.

She stared at him and then turned away.

"Don't you want to have children?" Robert was amazed at how anxiously he awaited her reply. He'd told himself he was content with Penelope as his only child, but the thought of making a child with Sydney filled him with intense longing.

"I would like to have children but..." Instead of finishing her sentence, she shrugged. Then, in an obvious attempt to change the subject, she asked, "Will they release Penny at seven in the morning?"

Robert allowed the change of topic, but he stored the hope of children with Sydney in the back of his mind. "Probably seven or eight o'clock, though I may ask the doctor to make it at six, if he can. And ask him not to reveal the change of time." He rolled his eyes in disgust. "Obviously there's a leak or no one would know we were here at the hospital."

"Do you think we'll be able to get away without being followed?"

"Yes, if the doctor will keep our departure time secret. I'll have to talk to him when there aren't any nurses around."

"You're assuming the leak is a woman."

"Sydney, are you a feminist?" he asked with a grin. Somehow he couldn't picture her with a sign at a protest march.

"I believe women should be paid as much as men

for honest work. And I don't believe only women are gossips.''

"You're right, but it's usually the lowest paid who are willing to sell information.''

"Oh.''

He had the urge to lean over and capture her stubborn lips with his, teasing them into passion—but he could tell she wouldn't accept such persuasion.

WHEN THE SUPPER TRAYS were brought, the three of them shared their meal. Penelope seemed to be recovering rapidly, and she sat up in bed to eat, reminding her father that she should get ice cream for dessert.

As usual, when the Duke of Hereford requested ice cream, it appeared at once. Enough for all three. Sydney enjoyed the treat, but she was tiring again.

The strain of worrying about the other two, and their privacy, as well as Penelope's recovery, was exhausting. In addition, the dowager duchess was a concern.

After watching an hour of television with the other two, Sydney stood.

"Robert, I think I'll spend the night at the bed-and-breakfast. Since Penelope is doing well, we should all get a good night's sleep.''

"You're going to leave me here?'' Penelope asked, her eyes widening.

"Sweetie, your dad's here, not to mention two security guards outside your door. I'm going to need to be awake tomorrow to drive safely.''

"But you won't leave without us, will you?" the child said, her eyes and voice pleading.

"Of course not. I'm going to deliver you to your cousin's ranch, like I promised. Okay?" She wanted to give in to Penelope's unspoken plea but it was time to begin distancing herself from the two of them.

"I don't like you going back on your own," Robert said, standing and putting his hand on her arm.

"Robert, I'm an adult. Besides, no one cares about me, so they won't notice if I slip out."

He turned her to face him. "The press may not care about you, but I can assure you Penelope and I do. Right, Pen?"

"Righto, Dad. We love you, Sydney." The child beamed at her.

She noticed that Robert didn't agree with his daughter. Not that she expected an avowal of love.

"I love you, too, sweetie, and I'll see you in the morning." After sending Penelope a smile, she pulled away from Robert and headed for the door.

Robert followed, giving her the chance to whisper, "I'll be here at six. Shall I pull up at the front door and keep the motor running?" Her words sounded silly, as if they were planning a bank heist instead of checking out of a hospital.

"I'll call you after I talk to the doctor. Are you sure you should go?"

When she looked at his eyes—at the open invitation she saw there—she knew she'd never been more sure of anything. No matter how much she wanted to stay, she had to leave.

"WHAT HAPPENED, DAD? Why did Sydney go?"

"She needed to rest, Pen."

Penelope sank back against the pillows. "I know, but...she will come back tomorrow, won't she?"

"She said she would. I trust her." It was a comforting feeling to trust Sydney. He liked it.

"I don't ever want Sydney to leave us." She peeked from under her lashes at her father. "I love her. Like a mummy."

Here was the opening Robert had been looking for. He stepped to the side of the bed and picked up Penelope's small hand. "Would you like Sydney to be your mother?"

Penelope's eyes glowed with happiness. "Oh, yes, Dad. That would be super!"

"It isn't decided," he cautioned. "I have to discuss it with Sydney, but I believe she will accept an offer of marriage."

"And she would go back to England with us? And live with us forever and ever?"

"Yes," he agreed, a simple response that didn't begin to cover his reaction to Penelope's words. Forever and ever. He couldn't imagine a better future.

"When will you tell her?" Penelope asked, assuming that Sydney would have no choice.

"I don't know. I can't discuss such a thing in front of an audience, poppet."

"What audience?"

"You, love," he told her with a smile. "Ladies expect to be asked in private."

"You could go ask her right now!" Penelope reasoned. "She's alone at that place we were staying, isn't she?"

"But I can't leave you alone," he returned, even as the idea set his heart racing.

"Oh."

"Unless I requested a nurse to stay with you all night. Would you be all right if a nurse stayed here while you slept? I could talk to Sydney and then we'd pick you up in the morning." The more he thought about it, the more he liked that plan. "What do you think?"

Penelope twisted her mouth as she thought. "I'd rather have both of you here, but I want Sydney to be my mum." She paused as if considering her decision. "Okay. I'll sleep here with a nurse while you talk to Sydney. And then in the morning, we'll be a real family!"

"It may not happen quite that fast. We'll have to plan a wedding, you know," Robert warned her, but he couldn't hold back a smile.

"At the ranch? Shall we have a wedding at the ranch with Nana and everyone?"

"Why not?" The more he thought about his child's suggestion, the more he believed it was a plan.

An excellent plan at that.

Chapter Twelve

As tired as she was, Sydney couldn't settle down. She'd greeted Mrs. Wright and given her an update on Penelope's condition. Fortunately, the woman had held their rooms.

However, as soon as the landlady realized Robert wouldn't be coming back that night, she decided to rent out his room, so asked Sydney to move his belongings to her room.

As Sydney turned away to clear the other room, Mrs. Wright said, "Oh, I almost forgot. Carl called to see if you were here. He said to tell you he found out who was calling you on the CB. I didn't really understand 'cause everyone does that, but he said you'd know what he meant."

"Did he say who it was?"

"No, but he said he told him to leave you alone. Was there a problem?"

"Not any more. Thanks, Mrs. Wright." Sydney was relieved, of course, but she'd been concentrating on Robert and Penelope so much, she'd forgotten her problem. She hoped Carl was right. But if it happened again, she'd go back to Carl.

Only half an hour later, a couple had shown up on the doorstep and moved in.

Sydney had already had her shower, so she didn't mind sharing the bath with strangers. In fact, the most disturbing part of the entire thing had been repacking Robert's things.

"You're going to have to get used to being alone again," she reminded herself as she paced about the room. Thinking about Robert and Penelope would only lead to heartbreak. In two days, they would be at their destination, and Sydney would be back on the road, alone.

Even the threats on the CB didn't seem to matter anymore compared to parting from Robert.

She'd made the mistake of giving her heart to him—and to Pen.

As she made another turn across the small bedroom, a knock sounded on her door. Assuming it was Mrs. Wright, Sydney swung open the door, then gasped.

Robert stood before her, a smile on his face.

"Why are you here? Has something happened to Penny? Is she all right?"

"She's fine," he assured her even as he clasped her shoulders to move her back into the room. He closed the door behind them.

"Then why are you here?" she asked, too distracted by his sudden appearance to notice his touch.

"I'm here to see you."

"What if Pen wakes up during the night?"

"A nurse is staying with her until we pick her up in the morning. Besides, she wanted me to come."

"Oh." She didn't know what else to say. Why had he come?

"Why is my luggage in here?" Robert asked, looking over her shoulder.

"Oh, no! Mrs. Wright rented out your room because I told her you wouldn't be coming back. She's full up now. What are you going to do?"

A slow smile spread across his handsome features and he pulled her closer against him. "I have an idea," he murmured and then covered her mouth with his.

Sydney had warned herself that any more involvement with Robert would cause her pain. But his lips overrode that idea with pleasure so intense that she couldn't quite remember her warning. His hands caressed her back, pressing her ever closer, until her breasts were flattened against his hard frame. Every time she moved, she was filled with sensations from her head to her toes.

Suddenly her world consisted only of Robert's arms, and of her happiness at his touch. All the longing for love, for family, was centered in him. She wrapped her arms around his neck and opened to his touch, his taste. When his lips left hers to trail kisses down her neck, she whimpered.

"Want to hear my idea?" he whispered as one hand reached for the belt on her knee-length robe.

Before she could manage a response, the robe was on the floor.

"Wh-what idea?" She couldn't even remember that he'd mentioned an idea earlier. She couldn't remember anything with Robert's hand sliding beneath the T-shirt she slept in.

"Robert, I don't—" She gasped as flesh connected with flesh. Without conscious thought, she sought to touch him, too, her fingers going to the buttons on his shirt.

"We'll share," he muttered before his lips touched hers again, deepening the intensity building within her. She hungrily opened her mouth to him, eager to taste him.

"Mmmm," she agreed, having no idea what she was agreeing to. Nothing mattered but him, slaking her thirst for his kisses, touching him all over.

"I'm glad you agree," he whispered. Pulling back, he deftly stripped her T-shirt over her head—before she could even protest at the distance between them. Then his mouth returned to hers.

Having gotten several buttons undone, she slipped her hands inside his shirt, stroking the muscles there, sliding her fingers through his chest hair. Her actions must have pleased Robert because he shrugged out of his shirt.

Bare chest to bare chest was almost more than Sydney could stand. And yet it was not enough. Her fingers moved down his chest until they encountered his belt. But she was distracted by his hands moving to her breasts.

She was growing overheated from the sparks that seemed to arc from her skin to his. Their time spent together had built an intimacy that made touching reasonable, but her heavy breathing told her she was about ready to explode.

Robert stroked one breast, tightening it to attention, then turned to the other one. A longing seized her—a longing for completion, for a oneness that would tie them together forever.

Lifting her against him, he replaced his hands with his lips, caressing and teasing her. She clung to him. Ecstasy filled her. She'd yearned to belong, to be loved, to connect with another human being. Since her father died, she'd been so isolated, so lonely.

Robert and Penny had already eased the loneliness. Now, Robert was bringing her that peace of completion, satisfaction...excitement. She had trouble finding her breath as he slid her back down, his body rubbing against hers.

"Sydney," he murmured, when his mouth released hers. She didn't know what he was asking, but she didn't want him to stop. What if he asked her something she couldn't answer? Or gave the wrong answer?

She'd die if he left her now.

Unable to think, only to respond, her mouth returned to his as her hands slid down his chest to his belt buckle. Though she knew she should be shocked at her forwardness, she tugged the belt loose and unfastened his pants, pulling the zipper down over his taut erection.

"Easy, love," he whispered, pressing her against him, his hands cupping her bottom.

She half sobbed, her desire building, and rubbed against him. When she began pushing his pants and underwear down, he did the same to her, discarding the pink panties, her only remaining article of clothing.

Suddenly, he lifted her against him, his mouth still fastened to hers, and laid her on the bed, falling to her side as he wrapped her in his arms. Sydney couldn't think. Sensations filled her and hunger drove her, making it impossible to hold back.

When Robert pulled away, she called his name with such longing that he immediately kissed her again. "One moment, love. I want to protect you."

He reached for his trousers and drew a small packet from his pocket. As he was opening it, Sydney tried to remember why she'd told herself intimacy with Robert was a bad idea. A glimmer of something struck her just as Robert pulled her against him and kissed her again.

And the reason went right out of her head.

He scooped her under him, and she spread her legs, welcoming him to her, urging him to fill her. When he entered her, his mouth covered hers, his tongue imitating his body, surging into her. She welcomed him with greater joy than she'd ever known.

They were one, and she never wanted to be separated again.

Then he began to move, and she lost all thought, responding to sensations greater than any she'd ever experienced. Her fiancé had never stirred her as Robert was.

When they had both reached completion—draining, totally overwhelming completion—Robert slid to the side and pulled Sydney tightly against him.

She snuggled against him, never wanting to awaken from the most glorious dream she'd ever had.

ROBERT HELD SYDNEY'S soft body against him, trying to control the response that was already arousing him again. He was too stunned by his reaction to her to allow a repetition of their lovemaking.

But he couldn't turn her loose.

What had happened? He wasn't a novice at sex, but he felt as if he'd just made love for the first time in his life. Certainly the most important time.

Not that that meant he was in love. He'd sworn he'd never allow a woman that much power over him again. But it boded well for their union.

He remembered he'd leapfrogged an important part of his plan, the mention of marriage. "Sydney?" he whispered in her ear.

For some reason, she shook her head, burrowing into his chest as if she were hiding.

"My dear, I forgot to ask you to marry me. Will you?"

She went still, and Robert feared she'd stopped breathing.

"Sydney?"

She pushed away from him, a wild look on her

face, then rolled off the other side of the bed, searching for her robe.

"Sydney, what are you doing? You don't need to— You're beautiful. Why are you—"

"Why?"

He smiled. "Why do I think you're beautiful? Any man—"

"Why did you ask me to marry you?"

Her question, whispered in a voice full of raw pain, stopped him, erased his smile, made him sit up.

"Because we will make a wonderful family. I trust you, Sydney. And Pen loves you. She wants you for a mum." He added his most charming smile, one even his mother seldom resisted.

"But you don't love me." Her words weren't a question but a statement of fact.

"Sydney, love, I trust you. That's more important than such a fickle emotion as love."

SYDNEY HELD BACK a sob as she stared at the man she'd given herself to, heart and soul—not to mention body.

"You're wrong, Robert. Trust is important, but it's not enough." She knew how important love was. Her father had loved her mother, even when she hadn't deserved his love. That love had kept him faithful and caring, even when she'd gone into the nursing home.

Love had outlasted everything.

Trust couldn't have that power.

The only reason she might marry Robert would be

if he loved her. Even then, she probably shouldn't. He might suspect her of marrying him for money when he found out how much her mother's care cost. And that would destroy the trust he said he had in her. Besides, she wasn't duchess material.

"Sydney," Robert said, rising in all his naked glory and coming toward her. "You're wrong. We will be very happy together."

She backed away. "No, Robert, I can't marry you."

"That's a strange remark after what just happened."

She felt faint. What had just happened had been the most powerful event in her life. And her biggest mistake.

"It…it was an accident."

"An accident? No, I don't think so."

"I want you to go," she insisted as he reached out for her. If he touched her again, she wasn't sure she'd have the power to resist.

"Go where? You agreed to share, remember?"

She gasped as remnants of the conversation that started their lovemaking came back to her.

"We both need our rest if we're going to drive tomorrow," he added, watching her.

"I—I think you should fly. I'll take you to the airport in the morning—"

"You promised Penelope. Are you going to break your word to her?"

"It will be too embarrassing!"

"No, it won't. If you won't marry me…" He

paused as if expecting her to contradict him. When she said nothing, he continued, "Then we'll pretend tonight never happened."

His words depressed her even more. If he could even contemplate such a thing, their lovemaking hadn't affected him nearly as much as it had her.

"We can't share the bed."

"Neither of us have any place else to sleep. I'll keep to my side, but I'm exhausted." He let his body sag, as if he had no energy left.

Guilt filled her as she remembered how little sleep he'd gotten the night before. She stared at the bed where they'd just made love, wishing it were king-sized. When she looked back at him, she thought she saw an alert, hungry expression that disappeared almost at once. She wondered if she'd imagined it.

"Well? I need to rest, Sydney. We'll just pretend that nothing happened. We'll have to rise early. Did you ask Mrs. Wright for a wake-up call?"

He picked up his jockey shorts and pulled them on. Sydney watched greedily, angry with herself at how much she still wanted him. Was she insatiable?

And was she crazy enough to get back in the bed with him?

He climbed into the bed and pulled the covers over him, turning his back to her. "Good night."

Stunned by his complete change, she stared for several seconds before she found her T-shirt and panties and quickly pulled them on.

He hadn't moved.

Wrapping the robe over her bedclothes, she turned

off the light and tiptoed to the bed, never taking her
eyes off him. She lifted the covers, then stopped,
waiting to see if he moved.

Nothing.

Finally she slid beneath the covers and lay rigid
on the mattress, wondering if she'd lost her mind.

She'd definitely lost her heart.

ROBERT LAY IN the darkness, listening to her
breathing, feeling the tension in her body. When she
finally released a big breath and relaxed, he sent up
a silent prayer of thanks. He wasn't sure what he was
going to do, but he was determined he would not
lose Sydney.

Why wouldn't she be reasonable? They were
physically compatible, a sedate way to describe the
explosion that had occurred tonight.

An explosion that he was eager to repeat.

Penelope loved her and wanted her for a mum.

He had a lot to offer her.

He'd wear her down. He had forty-eight hours to
work on her. He'd make sure she understood how
much he was offering her.

And if that didn't work, he'd find another way.

SYDNEY HAD ASKED Mrs. Wright to awaken her at
five-thirty the next morning, planning to roll out of
bed, throw on her clothes and be on her way. But
that was before she'd gained a roommate.

She'd awakened shortly before five, finding herself

wrapped in Robert's arms. Slowly, barely breathing, she'd withdrawn from his touch.

Then she'd gathered up fresh clothes and run for the shower. Standing under the steaming water, she'd tried to wash away the memory of his hands on her skin, his kisses—but those memories were stronger than soap and water.

She suspected only time would dull the sensations. Maybe in fifty years she wouldn't remember and crave his touch.

Maybe.

As she opened the door to the bathroom, clad in her jeans and shirt, she startled Mrs. Wright, who'd been about to knock on her door.

"Oh! Oh, my, Syd, I had no idea you were already up. I've fixed some of my banana-nut muffins for breakfast. You want some?"

Relieved that the landlady hadn't aroused Robert, Sydney nodded. "Yes, please, and I'd like to buy some extras to take to the duke and his daughter. It will save us time if we don't have to stop for breakfast."

"No need to pay me. By the way, I received a call last night from someone asking when the duke would be checking his daughter out of the hospital."

"What did you say?" Sydney demanded, her voice harsh.

"I told 'em they should ask the hospital, not me. I'm not a doctor."

"Bless you, Mrs. Wright."

"No problem, child. You gather your stuff and

come get the muffins. If you have a thermos, I'll pour you some coffee, too.''

''I'll be down in a few minutes.''

Mrs. Wright toddled back down the hall, but Sydney waited until she was completely out of sight before opening her door. Then, unable to postpone the dreaded moment any longer, she slipped into the room.

Robert was still sleeping. She moved to his side of the bed and stared down at his handsome face. He was every woman's dream: titled, wealthy, charming.

And she'd turned him down.

Because she knew she wasn't *his* dream. She'd always wanted someone to love her as her father had loved her mother. It hadn't taken long to find out that her fiancé wasn't that man. And she'd come to believe no man would love as her father had.

Should she settle for trust? Somehow she was sure she'd never love another man as she loved Robert. Could such an unequal match last? Unequal in social status, finances, even location—and, most of all, unequal in emotion.

Her eyes filled with tears that she refused to let fall. No, she couldn't share her bed, her life, with a man who didn't love her. However much she wanted to.

''Robert,'' she called softly, avoiding touching him.

His eyes popped open, but he didn't move his head. ''Yes?''

''It's five-thirty. You have twenty minutes before

we have to leave. I'll go settle the bill with Mrs. Wright and have muffins and coffee in the truck for you."

Without waiting for his response, she scooped up her belongings and Penelope's suitcase and left the room. After stowing away their things in the cab, she pulled out the thermos so Robert would have coffee.

She already knew he faced the morning better after a cup of coffee. Perhaps he preferred tea and had switched to coffee because he was in America. That thought surprised her, but it also showed her she didn't know him as well as she thought she did.

After all, they'd only known each other four or five days now. Surely he would be easy to forget. She'd lived twenty-six years without him in her life. But somehow, she wasn't convincing herself.

After a trip to Mrs. Wright's kitchen to pay the bill and collect the promised breakfast plus three small containers of orange juice, Sydney returned to her truck to wait.

She felt more comfortable there, more in control. And she desperately needed to feel in control. She intended to persuade Penelope that flying to the ranch would be best. But she didn't think she'd succeed.

Or was it that she secretly didn't want to succeed? Was she still reluctant to be parted from her English duo? Yes, she admitted with sadness.

She knew the inevitable was coming. But she wanted to delay it as long as possible.

Robert strode from the house, looking as neat and

unwrinkled as he always did. You would think he had one of those manservants following after him.

"Ready?" he asked as he swung into the passenger's seat.

Sydney didn't answer or look at him. She put the truck in gear.

"Have you taken care of the bill at the hospital?" she asked, hoping to keep what conversation they had on a impersonal level. "The business office probably won't be open this early in the morning."

"I visited with them last evening before I returned to Mrs. Wright's. What smells so delicious?"

She believed he was deliberately changing the subject, but it didn't bother her. She had no desire to discuss last night, either. "Mrs. Wright's muffins. There's coffee in the thermos. You know where I keep the cups."

He got up and found the cups, filling two, one for each of them. "Here."

"Thanks," she muttered, keeping her eyes on the road.

There was no more talk. What could they say?

In Sydney's mind, they'd made a colossal mistake, one that couldn't be corrected. Robert thought they could pretend it had never happened.

Hah!

"Shall I go to the front of the hospital?" She didn't think that would be the best choice, but it was Robert's decision.

"No. Go to the emergency entrance. It's always

open and hopefully no one will be watching for us there."

She did as he asked. As soon as she stopped, he opened his door. "We'll hurry. Be ready to leave as soon as we appear."

Nodding her head, she watched as he sprinted for the door. She sat numbly, staring at the door—losing track of time—until he strode out with a blanket-wrapped Penelope in his arms.

Chapter Thirteen

Sydney scooted across the cab, opened the door and waited for Robert to hand Penelope up into her arms. Surprised to discover the child was still asleep, she put her in the bed and tucked the sheet around her.

"Is she all right?" she whispered to Robert as he joined her.

"Of course. Why would you think she wasn't?"

"Well, she hasn't woken up." She turned to stare at Penelope as she continued sleeping.

"Pen sleeps soundly. You don't have to whisper," he assured her with a grin. "Now, let's…how do you Americans say? Move it?"

For the first time since last night, she smiled. "Yes, we'll move it."

She was already on the main highway, pressing the accelerator down, when she remembered to suggest the airport. "Are you sure you don't want to go to the airport?"

Though she kept her eyes on the road, she could feel Robert's gaze raking her. "Why would you ask that?"

She swiftly looked to see if he was teasing, then turned back to the highway. "I would've thought the reason was obvious."

"Not to me."

"We made a mistake, Robert. I think it makes everything awkward."

"A mistake? Is that what you call our making love?"

"We had sex. Love...love is different."

"Good show we didn't make love, then, because if it had been any more powerful, I might not have survived it."

Sydney tightened her lips and pressed the accelerator a little harder. She didn't want to discuss what had happened between them.

"We're riding with you, unless you kick us out, Sydney. After all, you promised Pen. What would she think if she woke up and discovered you'd broken your promise and not even said goodbye?"

Swallowing, Sydney whispered, "We have to part company anyway. It might be easier that way."

"No."

An uncompromising answer that left Sydney with nothing to say.

Movement behind her drew her attention. Penelope, a frown on her face, was sitting on the edge of the bed. "Why did you say that?"

"What, sweetie?" Sydney asked cautiously.

"That we have to part company. Dad said—"

"Um, Pen, I'll explain later," Robert hurriedly interrupted.

"But I want Sydney to be my mum!"

Robert started to speak, but Sydney beat him to it. "Sweetie, I'm not the duchess type. I wear jeans, remember? I eat fast food, not candlelight dinners. My friends are other truckers, not ladies and gentlemen."

"But—" Penelope began in protest.

Again Robert stopped her. "We'll work out something, Pen. But I need a little time. Now, how about some breakfast? We've got some great muffins and orange juice for you."

AFTER PENELOPE HAD her breakfast, Robert set up the television and let her watch cartoons the rest of the morning.

But the tension didn't ease with Penelope awake. Her impassioned plea for Sydney to be her mum ran through Sydney's head over and over again. When lunch drew near, Robert suggested they find somewhere to stop, allowing Penelope not only to eat but also to do a little walking.

"Do you mean somewhere other than a truck stop?"

"No, I'm not eliminating your normal kind of stop. Wherever you choose will be quite acceptable."

He added a charming smile that made her stomach roll with longing.

"We're entering Montana. I'll stop at the first place we see. We're making good time, so if there isn't a good place for her to exercise, we can take her to the nearest park.''

''Righto. That sounds like a good plan.'' He turned back to the child. ''How does that sound to you, Pen?''

He received no answer, because Penelope was watching another episode of *Sesame Street.* ''When she's recovered from her operation, I'm going to turn that thing off for at least a month.''

''A good idea,'' she agreed with a smile. Then she pointed at a billboard. ''There's a truck stop in five miles.''

''All right.'' He undid his seat belt and went to the bed. ''Time to get your shoes on, poppet.''

When they arrived at the busy restaurant, they went to an empty booth in the back. Their waitress barely gave them a second look. Too many patrons were demanding her attention.

The two adults joined Penelope in her choice of hamburger and fries.

''We call them chips in England, Sydney. Have you ever had chips?'' Penelope asked, munching on her fries.

''No, I haven't, Pen. I've read a lot of books about England because I plan to visit it someday.''

Robert turned to look at her. ''Perhaps we could talk you into a visit soon. You could stay with us.''

''No. No, I've already told you I can't take off work right now. I have financial obligations.'' She took a bite of her hamburger.

''But, Sydney, if you came to visit, I could show

you my pony. His name is Mouse,'' Penelope said eagerly.

Sydney just smiled and chewed.

"And I have some things to show you, too,'' Robert added, a twinkle in his eye that unnerved her.

Swallowing, she muttered, "Maybe someday.''

"And ladies don't chase Dad in England. Well, not much,'' Penelope added.

"How long are you staying at your uncle's ranch?'' Sydney asked, desperate to change the subject.

"I don't know. Dad?''

"Several weeks. Liz is scheduled to go into the hospital Monday. We'll stay until everyone is settled in again.''

"Will you be there Monday, Sydney? To see the baby?'' Penelope asked.

"No. I'll have to leave Sunday morning.''

"Oh.'' There was a sad look on her face.

"Eat your lunch, sweetie, so we can go play at a park.''

"We have time?''

"Yes, we do. We're going to take two days to get to your uncle's ranch. The doctor said you'd be okay if we didn't travel too far each day—and you stayed on the bed.'' Sydney smiled at her and ignored Robert. She forced herself to take another bite, but the little she'd eaten sat in her stomach like a load of rocks.

"At least no one is showing any interest in us,''

Robert murmured as Penelope turned her attention back to her lunch.

"We're fortunate they're so busy. Besides, it's been several days since your picture was in the paper."

"Are you saying my face isn't memorable?" he teased.

"Robert!" she protested, then blushed as he grinned at her.

"It's all right, love. I'll stop teasing if you'll eat your lunch. After our walk I intend to drive so you can take a nap."

"You certainly will not. I don't need to rest." She had no intention of getting into a bed anywhere near the Duke of Hereford.

He smiled as if he knew something she didn't— but said nothing.

When they'd finished their lunch, they headed for the cash register to pay. Penelope decided to look for a new book to read in the truck.

"Oh! Look, Dad! It's a picture of Sydney! Can I have a copy? I don't have a picture of Sydney."

Sydney whirled around and stared in horror at a tabloid newspaper, the front page filled with a picture of her and the headline saying she'd caught the duke. She hadn't even realized her picture had been taken. "Oh, no!" she moaned.

"It *is* her!" the waitress shouted as she leaned over Penelope to stare at the paper.

"Who is it?" a trucker shouted from several booths back.

''The lady who caught that duke. Ain't she lucky!''

Several people crowded around the three of them, and Sydney felt a momentary panic. Suddenly, a strong arm wrapped itself around her.

''Stand back, please. You're going to scare my child,'' he ordered firmly. Pulling them both in front of him, he threw down a twenty that more than covered their bill, and ushered them out the door.

''Wait!'' a shrill voice called out. ''If she's the one that caught him, then that must be the duke!''

Robert swept Penelope up against one shoulder and clutched Sydney with his other hand as he hurried them to the truck.

''Are they coming after us?'' Sydney asked as they reached the cab and she struggled to unlock the door.

''No, not at all. I guess there's no reason to pursue me if you've already caught me, Sydney. Are you both all right?'' Robert asked.

Surprised, Sydney looked over her shoulder. Robert was right. No one was coming after them. ''Then it wasn't necessary to run?''

''Oh, I'm not sure. But I had no desire to discuss our, uh, recent history with strangers.''

Sydney's eyes widened as she took in his words. ''No. Of course not.'' She scrambled up the side of the cab and disappeared from view.

ROBERT SUGGESTED they find a hotel for the night, since there was no need to drive until late.

Sydney, however, seemed reluctant to appear in public now that she knew her picture was spread across America. This was a new experience for her, not one she'd easily get accustomed to.

"But I didn't get to stay in the last hotel," Penelope complained. "I had to go to the hospital."

"Yes, well, I suppose we can stop at a hotel, but I'm afraid we'll be recognized."

"I've got a quite brilliant idea," Robert suggested. "We'll send Pen in to register."

Penelope cheered, not realizing her father was teasing. Sydney scolded him and assured the child she would not be going into a hotel alone.

"Never mind, Pen," Robert said as Penelope complained. "We'll find a hotel and I'll register us. Under assumed names."

"What's an assumed name, Dad?" Penelope asked.

"We make up a different name from our own and introduce ourselves as, say, the queen of England and her entourage."

His outrageousness made even Sydney chuckle.

"I want to be someone," Penelope decided. "Who can I be?" Before anyone else could speak, she shouted, "I know, I know, I shall be Big Bird."

"Hmm, no, not yellow enough," Sydney returned, grinning.

"There's a likely hotel," Robert said, pointing to a stately building. They had recently entered the city limits of Billings.

"But it's too early to stop for the evening. We can cover a lot more distance before—"

"No, it's been a long day. I want us all to relax. Pull in here."

Sydney did as he requested.

"Let me out at the front door and you and Penelope go park. I'll wait for you in the lobby."

"But what if someone recognizes you?"

"Don't worry about it."

After Robert got out of the cab, Sydney followed his directions, although she didn't think stopping off at the most expensive hotel in Billings was a good idea.

"Dad picked a good hotel, Sydney. I know it will have room service. Will you ask Dad if I can have some more ice cream?"

Penelope's request teased Sydney out of her worries. "I think it's a good thing you're traveling in the summer, or you might freeze from all the ice cream you're eating."

Penelope giggled.

Once the truck was parked, Sydney helped Penelope to the ground. "Can you walk all right?" she asked anxiously as Penelope rubbed her side.

"Yes, if we go slow."

When they reached the door, a smartly dressed doorman opened it for them, bowing low.

"Do you think he knows Dad's a duke?" Penelope whispered.

Sydney, with a quick look over her shoulder, reassured the child. "No, I think he opens the door for everyone."

Penelope spied her father chatting with a man dressed in a dark suit. She tried to hurry and then slowed down again. "Ooh. That hurt."

"Take it easy, Pen." Sydney wanted to hurry, however, out of the open area. She felt all eyes were staring at her.

"There you are," Robert said, scooping Penelope up into his arms and then bending over to kiss Sydney's cheek.

She jerked back and stared at him.

"Good evening, my lady. I hope you and your husband have a lovely stay," the man in the dark suit said, bowing slightly.

"My wife is overcome with your kind welcome. If you'll excuse us, we must tuck Penelope up for her nap," Robert said, and guided his two stunned female companions to the elevator.

WHAT WAS Robert thinking? Sydney asked herself.

Did he believe she would sleep with him again because she'd already done so? In front of his child?

She found herself in the elevator without remembering how she'd gotten there. As soon as the doors closed, however, she demanded, "What have you done?"

"Gotten us a lovely suite."

"I'm not talking about the accommodations! You told him we were married? And you told him who you are?"

"Yes, and paid extra for him to keep our location a secret. Now we can relax, order room service—"

"Sydney!" Penelope hissed from her father's shoulder.

"Um, Penelope wants more ice cream," Sydney responded to the prompt, frowning. Then she returned to the more pressing topic. "Robert, I won't—"

"You won't mind sharing with Penelope again, will you, my dear?"

Her gaze snapped to his face, only to discover that teasing twinkle in his eyes. "Share with Penelope?"

"Yes. I would've gotten a three-bedroom suite, but they didn't have one. Or, if you insist, I can sleep on a sofa in the living room—but I'd prefer a bed."

"No, I don't mind sharing," she mumbled, studying the carpet on the elevator floor. She realized he knew what she had thought and that he was laughing at her.

Of course he wouldn't be all that interested in sleeping with her again. After all, he was a duke. He was rich. He could have any woman in America *or* England. Except maybe the queen.

He handed her the key as the elevator opened. She stepped out onto the small landing, finding only one door. When she opened it, she understood why. The penthouse suite was huge and the outer walls were glass, with sheer drapes to dim the light.

"It's beautiful."

"Yes, quite. Well, poppet, which bedroom would

you prefer? You and Sydney,'' he added, slanting another teasing look at Sydney.

"Show them to me,'' Penelope insisted. Robert carried her to a door on the right side of the large living area, then across it to another door.

"Ooh, this one. It's pink and gold. Come see, Sydney. And it has a bed for each of us. The other one has only one bed, a huge one.''

In which Sydney immediately pictured Robert, sprawled beneath the covers, as he had been this morning. She drew a deep breath. "Yes, this room is perfect for us.''

"Dad, I don't need a nap. I've been resting in Sydney's bed all day,'' Penelope protested as Sydney turned down the covers.

Robert ignored his child's protest and put her down, but she grabbed his arm, then looked at Sydney. "Sydney, I need to talk to Dad. Will you go to the other room for a little while?''

Surprised, and a little hurt if truth be told, Sydney left the room, wondering if Penelope had already tired of her—just as her father surely would.

"Now, what is it, poppet?''

"Dad, I think you need to show Sydney she can be a duchess.''

"What are you talking about, Pen?''

"Remember what she said about wearing jeans, and not eating candlelight dinners?'' She clutched her father's shirt in her eagerness.

"Yes. But I—''

"If you bought her pretty things—a dress and perfume and all that stuff Mummy used to look nice—and had a candlelight dinner for her, then she would know she could be a duchess."

Robert's eyes widened as he took in Pen's meaning. "But, love, Sydney doesn't need those things to be a duchess. She's beautiful in her jeans. And it's the heart that makes someone important. Not candle-lit dinners."

Penelope pulled him even closer.

"Dad, I don't want Sydney to go away. *Please* buy her pretty things so she'll stay."

"But, Pen, you don't want her to stay just because we buy her things, do you?" He'd had that kind of marriage before. He didn't want another one. Not that he believed for a moment that Sydney would marry him for money.

"Sydney's not like that, Dad. But she doesn't think she can be a duchess. Didn't you hear her?"

He remembered Sydney's words. Did Pen have it right? "You're a smart little blighter, aren't you, love. But are you sure?"

"Yes. And buy her roses. That's what they always bring on the telly. And pretty earrings."

Robert still wasn't convinced Penelope was right, but he decided her idea couldn't hurt. "You'll have to stay in your bedroom and go to bed early. Is that all right?"

"Sure. I'll do anything to have Sydney as my mum."

"All right. I'll get her to come keep you company while I do a little shopping."

"And this time, she'll say yes, won't she, Dad?"

Robert sighed. "I certainly hope so."

Chapter Fourteen

Robert asked Sydney to keep Penelope company while he ran a few errands. When she asked him if he was worried about being spotted, his answer surprised her.

"Now that they know about you, I think the notoriety will go away. If I can't marry them, those women won't have any interest in me." With a "cheerio," he left the room, leaving Sydney with her mouth open.

Once Penelope was tucked in her bed, Sydney lay down on the other one. *Sesame Street* was on television, the volume down low. Sydney closed her eyes, sure it would encourage Penelope to do the same.

That was her last thought before she fell asleep.

ROBERT RETURNED several hours later with a large number of packages, and their luggage carried by a porter. He asked the man to leave the bags by the front door. Then, after tipping him and sending him away, Robert tiptoed over to the bedroom door and opened it carefully.

Both ladies were sound asleep, their faces relaxed. Penelope even had a smile on her lips—but Sydney was frowning.

He was tempted to tease those lips into a smile. Only he knew he wouldn't be able to stop. His control around Sydney was getting weaker and weaker.

Closing the door, he turned back into the living room, pacing across the floor. Time was running out. He hoped Penelope's idea worked.

If it didn't, Sydney was going to leave him.

How desperate was he, taking advice from a six-year-old? He'd done as she asked, however. Everything Sydney would need to transform herself into Cinderella was in the bags by the door. He'd ordered an elegant candlelight dinner to be served about Penelope's bedtime.

Tonight he would show Sydney she would be perfect in his world.

MAISIE ANSWERED the phone, as usual, but she was in the middle of cooking Liz's favorite meal. "Hello? Oh, Robert. Yes, your mother is here somewhere. Just a moment."

She hurried to the stairs and called. "Mary Margaret? It's Robert."

As soon as she heard the telephone picked up upstairs, she went back to her cooking.

"Robert? Is Penelope well?"

"Yes, Mother, Penelope is recovering nicely."

"Good show. By the way, Miss Thomas is quite attractive." She could almost hear her son stiffen.

"How do you know?"

"I bought that awful tabloid. Most interesting story. Of course, I didn't believe it. I know you won't let anyone trap you into marriage again." When Robert didn't immediately respond, she grinned.

"No one has trapped me," Robert finally said. "In fact, I may need to trap Sydney. It appears my title doesn't appeal to *every* woman in America."

"Robert, surely you don't intend to marry this woman. Her family is unknown. After all, you have to be careful who you choose to be Penelope's new mother."

"Sydney will be the best mother Pen could have, and I'll thank you to keep your opinions to yourself when we arrive. I don't want Sydney frightened away."

"But at least allow me to explain the duties of a duchess. You have to think of the title."

"No, Mother, I have to think of my happiness and Pen's. And Sydney will make us happy. I wanted to warn you—before we arrive tomorrow—to make her feel welcome."

"I know how to be a hostess."

"Yes, but I want you to welcome Sydney into the family."

"Hmmm. We'll see. I must approve her first."

After several more remonstrations from Robert, she hung up the phone and turned to face her only daughter-in-law, Pete's wife, Liz.

"What are you up to, Mary Margaret?" Liz asked as she leaned back against the pillows, her four-year-old daughter beside her, holding a book for her to read.

"Why, Liz, whatever do you mean?"

"I mean it sounded to me like you were discouraging Robert from remarrying."

The dowager duchess smiled widely. "You won't mind if this little boy isn't the heir to a dukedom, will you?" she asked, patting her daughter-in-law's hugely protruding stomach.

"Mind? I'd be delighted, you know that. But if that's what you're hoping, why discourage Robert?"

The older lady crossed her arms and smiled again. "Because if I encourage him, he'll run in the opposite direction. Reverse psychology, my dear."

ROBERT WAS WATCHING the evening news on television when the bedroom door opened and Sydney emerged. "Have a nice nap?" he asked, smiling.

"Yes. I didn't mean to sleep so long."

"That's all right. You needed the rest." He swallowed, suddenly nervous about the evening's plan. "Um, while I was out, I picked up a few things for you." He gestured to the bags he'd moved to one of the chairs.

"What are you talking about? What things?"

"I thought you might enjoy a little pampering tonight. There's a dress to wear, some lotions, some, uh, undies."

She stared at him, her eyes narrowing. His misgivings grew. He watched her as she crossed the room to open the bags.

Looking up at him, she folded the tops of the bags back in place. "I hope you saved the receipts so you can get your money back," she said evenly.

"Why would I want to return them?"

"Because you've wasted your money. I'm not going to change."

"I don't want you to change, Sydney. I'm quite pleased with you the way you are."

She stood stiff and proper against the wall, glaring at him. "Of course you are, Robert. That's why you bought all this...these things. Because you don't want me to change."

"Sydney, I wanted to thank you for all you've done for us. If you want to wear jeans while we dine by candlelight, I certainly don't mind. In fact, you may dine naked if you prefer." Just the thought of that picture stirred a response in him.

As if reading his thoughts, she protested, "We weren't going to talk about last night, remember? You said we'd just forget it."

"Sydney—" he began, unsure what to say. His idea of forgetting their incredible lovemaking had been stupid, but he'd been desperate.

"You didn't have to buy things to convince me that I'm not proper duchess material, Robert. I wasn't going to try to force you to marry me." Her anger seemed to increase as she stood there. "Did you think I was dumb enough to think I'd fit into your life? Look at me!"

"Sydney, you're wrong."

"Oh, right! Like I'd believe you after you went out and bought all that for me!"

"He bought it because of me," a little voice said.

Both of them turned to the bedroom door to find Penelope leaning against it.

"How are you feeling, Pen?" Sydney asked, putting aside her anger as she rushed to the child's side.

"Sydney, Dad bought you those things because I asked him to. I wanted you to know that you'd make a great duchess," Penelope said, tension on her face. "Dad said you didn't need pretty things to make a good duchess. I'm the one who insisted. Don't be mad at Dad."

Sydney fell to her knees beside his daughter. "Sweetie, you've got to forget about me being your mummy. I wouldn't fit in."

"You fit in with us. Doesn't she, Dad?"

Robert nodded but wisely kept his silence. He thought his daughter might better say what was in his heart.

"That's because you and your dad were traveling incognito."

"Then you can be incognito with us!" Penelope proclaimed.

Sydney turned to Robert for help. He gave Pen a crooked grin. "If Sydney married us, poppet, she couldn't be incognito. But it wouldn't matter. She'd be a perfect duchess."

"Robert, how can you say that? Look at me!"

"Oh, I am, love, I am. All you're talking about

are clothes—the easiest things in the world to change. What can't be changed is what's in here," he said solemnly, tapping his chest. "You have the heart of a duchess."

Tears filled her eyes and he wanted to cross the room and sweep her into his arms. But he didn't move.

"Please put on the pretty things Dad bought. I want to see you all dressed up. I'm going to go to bed early, too, so you and Dad can have— You *did* order candlelight, didn't you, Dad?"

Her sudden switch to a stern tone made Robert laugh. What a child! "Of course I did. Just like you ordered." Then he turned to a bemused Sydney. "I'm afraid we must follow orders, my dear. You know how patients are."

Sydney considered his words. "I would enjoy a lovely dinner, though I think Penelope should join us. But, Pen, it won't make any difference. You do understand that, don't you?"

"Will you just try? For me?"

Robert knew she couldn't hold out against Penelope's pleading look. He kept quiet, letting his child fight his battle for him.

"I'll have dinner, of course, but—"

"And you'll wear the pretty things Dad bought you? I want to see you in a dress."

Sydney took a step back. "I don't think—"

Time to intervene. "It seems a harmless enough request, Sydney. Unless you have a great aversion to dresses."

"No, of course not, but—"

"Good. Then take the bags and go get ready. Our dinner will be here in about an hour. Does that give you enough time?"

"Yes, but—"

"I'll help," Penelope said, beaming.

"Good." Robert moved over to Sydney's side and whispered, "If you don't mind, she can watch from the bed. It will keep her from tiring."

Having switched Sydney's attention from herself to the child, he urged the two into their bedroom and shoved the packages in after them.

Then he sat down to await his duchess.

WHEN THE SACKS were emptied on her bed, Sydney stared, unable to believe Robert had purchased so much. Just touching the silk dress, in forest green, made her feel more elegant.

"Your father—I can't...."

"Didn't he buy the right size?" Penelope asked.

"Yes, it looks like it's the right size, but it's much too expensive. I'll never be able to pay him back."

"Sydney, you don't understand," the child protested. "These are gifts from Dad and me." As if that explained everything, the little girl began to dig through the pile of purchases. "He was supposed to buy you bubble bath. Oh, here it is."

"Bubble bath?"

"It makes you smell good. I could use some of it after you," Penelope suggested, a speculative look on her face. "I like to take baths with bubbles."

Sydney seldom allowed herself such a treat. And never in the summer when she was driving. "Well, maybe we should both take a bubble bath. We wouldn't want the gift to go to waste."

"And Dad bought you some new pink underwear, too. It's very pretty." She picked up the bra, a scrap of delicate lace. "When will I get to wear one of these?"

Sydney smiled. "Not for a few years, Penny. And don't be in a hurry. Life is less complicated at your age." She took the article from Penelope's hand, blushing at the thought of Robert choosing such intimate apparel as a bra and matching bikini panties.

It reminded her of last night.

Oh, no. They were supposed to forget last night.

In a few million years.

Which reminded her of how alone, how lonely she would be when Robert and Penelope left her.

Why not enjoy this evening? Why not pretend for one evening, that she was on their level? Could live life as they did? Could be happy with them.

Suddenly hiding her misgivings, she threw herself into the Cinderella spirit. Tonight she'd been given the perfect ball gown, the perfect prince, the perfect evening. Like last night, the memories would have to last her a lifetime. So she was going to do her best to make them perfect.

An hour later, when Robert knocked on the bedroom door to tell her their dinner had arrived, Sydney took one last, wondering look in the mirror.

"What do you think?" she asked Penelope in a whisper.

"Turn around," Penelope ordered from her bed.

Sydney approached the bed. She was wearing the green silk gown, floor length, with a draped neckline that dipped low in front. Gold earrings sparkled in her ears, drawing attention to the curtain of reddish-brown hair that fell loose down her back.

"I like those things in your hair."

"Your father thoughtfully included decorative combs. In fact, I can't think of anything he left out. He must, uh, have a lot of experience about what ladies like."

"I think Nana told him," Penelope said, nodding solemnly.

Somehow, Sydney didn't think his mother taught him about the expensive lingerie he'd purchased for her. And she didn't want to know how he knew about it.

"Um, probably. Will I do?"

"Oh, Sydney, you look beautiful. Prettier than any of those other ladies who want to marry Dad."

Sydney bent forward and kissed Penelope's cheek. "You're prejudiced, but I like it."

"Sydney, are you coming out?" Robert called.

"I'm coming," she called, then drew a deep breath. It was time for Cinderella to go to the ball.

ROBERT STOPPED BREATHING when the door opened and Sydney stood before him. In jeans, she was a sexy lady. In silk, with her glorious hair spread across her shoulders, the gown faithfully outlining her curves, she was an elegant, beautiful woman.

"Isn't she pretty, Dad?" Penelope called from her bed.

"She's exquisite," he said softly, his gaze never leaving Sydney.

She blushed and looked away.

"Pen, I have your dinner here. And, as a surprise, a Disney video. You can watch the real Cinderella."

It only took minutes to settle Penelope. Then Robert led Sydney into the living room. A table holding their dinner was set up by the floor-to-ceiling window, candles glowing in its center, surrounded by the roses Penelope had ordered.

"You really did order candlelight," Sydney said with a sigh.

"I was under strict orders," he reminded her, chuckling.

He led her to the table, pulling out her chair for her. She sank gracefully into it and he rounded the table to join her. Crisp green salads were already in place.

"This is a little different from the truck stops we've been frequenting."

"Not really."

She looked at him questioningly.

"At those meals, like this one, I've dined with the most beautiful companion."

"Robert—" she protested, but there was a smile on her lips.

They ate their salads in silence. Then Robert uncovered the beef burgundy he'd ordered. When he resumed his seat, Sydney asked him to tell her about his brother and his wife.

He talked through most of the rest of dinner, making an amusing tale of Liz's performance as a counterfeit princess when she first met Pete, his brother. He downplayed his mother's involvement, but Sydney figured it out.

"Your mother was trying to arrange a marriage of convenience for your brother?"

"She thought she was doing the right thing. She thought Pete would resent my inheriting the title."

"And did he?"

Robert smiled. "No. He's happy on the ranch."

"Are you happy having a title?"

He studied her. "I could be."

"If you had—?"

"Someone to share my life."

"Robert—"

"It's time for dessert," he said abruptly, changing the subject. He didn't intend to allow her to refuse him.

"I couldn't eat another thing," she protested, still watching him as if he might trick her.

He rose again and this time uncovered two slices of the most decadent-looking chocolate cake.

"How did you know my favorite?" she asked in surprise.

"Lucky guess. It happens to be my favorite, also. Try some."

Taking a bite, Sydney closed her eyes as the moist

cake and thick chocolate icing sprinkled with pecans slid across her tongue. "Mmmm, it's wonderful." She opened her eyes to find his intense gaze fixed on her lips. "Have you tried yours?" she hurriedly asked.

He immediately picked up his fork and took a bite. "Very good."

"Very rich."

"In the interest of maintaining our figures, how about a dance?"

Again he threw her off-stride. "A dance? Here?"

He crossed the room to switch the radio to a station that was playing a slow pop song. Then he returned to her side and extended a hand.

"I'm not a very good dancer," she protested.

He ignored her and took her hand, pulling her up from the chair. "I won't let you fall," he whispered in her ear as he clasped her in his arms.

Sydney shivered as she leaned against his hard body, loving the warmth that flooded her, the memories it reawakened of their exquisite loving. As his lips caressed her temple, that warmth turned to a raging hunger. She closed her eyes, hoping to resist her urges.

"Ah, Sydney, you lied. You dance beautifully," Robert said, smiling against her forehead.

"Robert, we're scarcely moving," she said, her voice breathless. She couldn't take a deep breath when his arms were around her.

"The best kind of dancing," he assured her.

"Don't you know a man dances so he can hold his woman? Not because he thinks he's Fred Astaire."

His woman. She squeezed her eyes tightly shut to escape the pain of longing that filled her.

He pulled her a little closer, even though she hadn't thought there was any space left between them. Now, though, she felt his body with every inch of hers. Neither the silk gown nor the lacy underwear were barriers to his hard muscles.

Taking her hand that he held, he laid it on his shoulder, then wrapped both his arms around her. "Americans dance like this. I've seen them. Jolly good show, I think."

"Not...not often. Robert, I think you shouldn't—"

She never finished her protest because his lips covered hers. They stopped moving altogether, except for Sydney's heart thumping double-time in her chest.

With the last remnant of common sense, she pulled her mouth away. "I think I need some more chocolate cake."

Her choices were eating cake—or dragging him to the floor and ravishing him.

Though he released her, she could feel that he did so reluctantly. "Okay. A little more chocolate cake."

He seated her at the table again. "I didn't realize the cake was *such* a favorite," he teased.

Obviously he hadn't believed her ploy. "I don't get to eat such wonderful desserts very often," she assured him with a decorous smile.

He smiled in return. "Our lives really aren't all that different, you know."

The non sequitur startled her. "What are you saying?"

"Neither of us indulge in chocolate cake every day. We both have jobs to do and we do what's required of us. We take care of our loved ones."

He paused as if expecting her to say something, but Sydney sat silently watching, like a rabbit mesmerized by a snake.

"And we're both lonely," he added softly.

Pain ripped through her, but she couldn't admit how right he was. Picking up her fork, she took another bite of cake. The sugary confection served as a distraction only. But thankfully, the romantic mood had been broken.

"I think you and I could combine forces and both be happy," Robert urged, leaning forward. "Sydney, Penelope wants you for her mummy."

What could she say? *I'll be her mummy but not your lover?* She knew she wouldn't resist filling Robert's bed if she were constantly around him. She wasn't strong enough.

"A marriage can't be built on a child's needs."

"What about my needs?"

She flashed him an angry glare. He wasn't playing fair. "Robert! We weren't going to discuss last night, remember?"

"I wasn't discussing our lovemaking. I was discussing my loneliness," he assured her, a smile on his face. "But I don't mind telling you last night was wonderful."

"You should go out more, find the right woman to marry," she said desperately, ignoring his words.

"I have."

"Robert, you know I'm not the right woman. You're a nobleman, for goodness' sake."

"That's the good thing about being a nobleman," he assured her. "You can do whatever you want, as long as you don't break the law."

"But I have responsibilities here."

"I'll take care of your responsibilities. We can move your mother to a nursing home in England."

"And then I'll be no better than the others who have tried to marry you."

"What do you mean?" he asked.

Sydney couldn't believe he had to ask. "You've complained about the women who would marry you for your money. Then you suggest I do the same."

"The same? Sydney, letting me take care of your mother is not marrying me for my money. Those other women want furs, jewels, cars, but they're not willing to give anything back in return."

"You make marriage sound like some kind of bartered arrangement." She wanted to get up and run away, but he kept her in her place with his gaze.

"It is. A man takes a wife to be a helpmeet—to offer comfort and loving, to have children. In return, he cares for her, provides for her."

"What about love?"

"That's a very overrated emotion. It clouds the

issues. But I know you will love Pen. And we've proved how compatible we are.''

Her heart sank. He had tempted her with his arguments, letting her think that he might love her, that they might make a future together.

But he didn't love her. He didn't believe in it. One day, he might meet someone who inspired the kind of emotion her father had felt for her mother. And then her world would end.

"I can't!" she gasped and jumped up from the table. Before he could stop her, his Cinderella ran away, leaving not even a shoe behind.

Chapter Fifteen

"Well, Dad? Did Sydney agree?" Penelope asked, shaking her father as he lay sleeping.

He groggily opened his eyes. Sleep had not come easily the night before, and he would've enjoyed a few more hours. "Not exactly."

"But, Dad," Penelope protested, "what happened? She looked like a duchess."

"I know," he said gently, seeing in his mind the vision he'd danced with the night before. "I haven't given up, poppet. I think Sydney cares about us. And we have until tomorrow morning."

Penelope put her hands on her hips and stared at him. "Okay, Dad, but you'd better convince her," she insisted, stomping a foot—the poster child for noble arrogance. "If you don't, I'll never forgive you!"

Robert nodded in understanding. After all, if he didn't, he'd never forgive himself, either.

WHEN SYDNEY AWOKE, Penelope had already arisen, and she was alone. She told herself she was taking advantage of the luxury she'd never experienced, starting with another bubble bath.

In reality, she was hiding from the temptation of Robert Morris, the Duke of Hereford. It was too tempting to surrender to his offer of marriage. She would be surrounded by luxury the rest of her life. The care of her mother would be taken on by Robert. She could have children, her own family.

Never again would she be alone.

But to marry for any reason but love was wrong. Love for both of those involved.

So she luxuriated in the hot water and worked on her resistance. When she finally came out of the bedroom, she was prepared to be friendly, but distant.

Robert immediately tested her resolve. Before she knew what he was doing, he pulled her into his arms and kissed her.

"Good morning, my dear," he said with a grin as he released her lips.

"G-good morning," she managed to reply as she pushed her way out of his embrace.

"I want a kiss!" Penelope called from the table.

Sydney hurried over to comply.

"Of course, sweetie." After brushing her lips against Penelope's soft cheek, she sat down beside her. "Is there any breakfast left for me?"

"Yes. Dad ordered lots."

"Here you are, Sydney," Robert said, coming to her side. He offered her a plate with pastries, and indicated several silver-domed dishes hiding scrambled eggs, bacon and sausage.

"There're strawberries, too," Penelope added.

"My favorite. I don't think we'll even need to stop for lunch if I eat all of this," she said to Penelope, doing her best to ignore the handsome hunk hovering over her.

"We won't need to stop for lunch anyway," Robert said. "I think we're only about three hours away from the ranch. Maisie will fix us lunch."

"Who is Maisie?"

"My brother's housekeeper."

"I thought he was married," Sydney commented as she ate.

"He is. Liz stays busy. There's a lot to do on a ranch, especially when there are small children. Their daughter is four and keeps everyone hopping."

"I didn't mean to imply…that is, I'm not used to having servants." She kept her gaze on her plate.

"Maisie isn't a servant. She's more like part of the family. Like Liz's mother, who lives with them, also. The two of them make life easier for everyone on the ranch."

"We have a housekeeper, too," Penelope chimed in. "And three maids. And my nanny."

"Yes, well, we'll talk about our staff another time," Robert said hastily.

Sydney had no intention of discussing their staff. With her appetite suddenly disappearing, she wiped her face with the linen napkin and stood.

"You can't have finished," Robert protested.

"Yes, I have. Shall we get started? I know Penny

is anxious to see her cousin again. Are you packed, Penny?"

"Yes, Sydney. Want me to help you pack?"

The child might not be much help with the packing, thought Sydney, but she'd ensure her protection against being alone with Robert. "That would be wonderful."

"Pen," Robert interrupted as both ladies headed to the bedroom, "I think you should watch the cartoons while you can. I'm not sure what kind of reception Sydney's telly will get in the mountains."

"But I promised Sydney."

"I'll help her if she needs assistance," Robert offered.

"That's all right. I can manage," Sydney said quickly. "I don't have much to pack."

As she spoke, Sydney suddenly realized she would be going to a millionaire's ranch in jeans and T-shirt. She didn't have a single dress or skirt or even a nice shirt to wear, except for what Robert bought her yesterday. Somehow, she didn't think floor-length silk would be appropriate, even if a dowager duchess was in residence.

"If we get to the ranch at lunchtime, I believe I can make Denver by dark. It would probably be best if I don't stay—"

"But, Sydney, you promised!" Penelope said, coming to her side and throwing her arms around her.

Sydney avoided Robert's stare as she smoothed several wisps of hair from Penelope's face.

"Sweetie, I don't think— I don't have anything to wear that—"

"Is that all you're worried about?" Robert demanded, stepping closer. "We're going to a ranch, Sydney, not the queen's ball."

Penelope buried her face in Sydney's stomach. "Please stay, Sydney. Please?"

Sydney knew she was going to feel awkward and ill at ease, but she couldn't say no to Penelope. "All right, sweetie, just until Sunday morning, though. I promised my scheduler I'd pick up my load on Monday morning."

"Maybe someone else can pick it up and you can stay as long as we do," Penelope suggested, beaming now that she'd received the reassurance she wanted.

Sydney bent over to kiss her forehead. "No, Penny. Sunday morning is it, I'm afraid. But maybe you and I can write to each other once you return to England."

Penelope pressed her cheek to Sydney again. "Okay," she agreed glumly.

None of them seemed satisfied with Sydney's suggestion.

ROBERT WAS RIGHT. They were approaching the ranch right at noon. He'd called before they left the hotel three hours ago to alert Maisie to include them for lunch.

Sydney was glad she wasn't pulling a load as she maneuvered the mountainous state. It also would have been tiring because she was having difficulty concentrating on her driving with her meeting with Robert's family fast approaching.

"Nana will be so glad to see us," Penelope said as Sydney turned into a one-lane hard-topped road and passed through a gate with a sign reading Palisades Ranch.

"I'm sure she will," Sydney agreed, trying to relax her tense shoulders.

"She'll be glad to see you, also," Robert added. "She's already commented on your beauty."

"How would she... Oh, no! She saw the newspaper?" Sydney turned horrified eyes on Robert.

She could tell he regretted his words, but he tried to soothe her. "She didn't believe the story, Sydney. It doesn't matter."

She shot him a dubious look, wishing she'd never promised Penelope she'd stay the night. As much as she wanted to be with these two, she would leave at once if she could.

By the time she'd stopped the truck, several people were on the back porch, visible from the space Robert had directed her to.

"Nana!" Penelope called as she waved.

Robert opened the door and Penelope, quite experienced now, scrambled down the side of the truck and started toward the porch. She was moving more slowly than normal, but her agility was improving every day.

"You are coming, aren't you?" Robert asked, watching Sydney.

Reluctantly, she nodded. "Yes, of course." With

shaking fingers, she opened her door and climbed down.

When she rounded the truck, Robert was waiting for her. Her cheeks flamed as he caught her hand and pulled her along with him to greet his family.

The dowager duchess—at least Sydney assumed that's who she was—had already hugged her granddaughter and offered Robert the same greeting. Sydney snatched her hand from him and stepped back.

Almost at once, however, he turned to her. "Mum, I want to introduce Sydney Thomas."

"How do you do, Miss Thomas?" the woman said, her voice cool. "I do appreciate the service you provided my son."

Sydney felt as welcome as a mosquito on a warm summer evening. "It was nothing, my lady."

The lady raised one eyebrow, as if surprised that Sydney had known how to address her—but she said nothing else.

Robert was now being hugged by a man who looked a great deal like him. After introducing his brother Peter, Robert led her to the porch where a beautiful and extremely pregnant lady awaited them, holding on to a four-year-old. It was Penelope who introduced her to Liz, Pete's wife, and their daughter, Stacy. Then, inside the spacious kitchen, she met Maisie and Liz's mother.

"I thought lunch would be ready," Robert said, looking at the bare table.

"A'course it is. You're eating in the dining room," Maisie assured him.

"The dining room? I thought you always had lunch in here."

Maisie shrugged her shoulders and didn't look at him. "Mary Margaret thought we should be more formal in honor of your guest."

Sydney's back stiffened. She knew how to translate the dowager duchess's decision. She wanted to know if Sydney knew how to behave.

"Is there somewhere I could wash up?" she asked calmly.

"Of course," Liz said, about to get up.

Several people protested her moving, and her husband said, "You're not even supposed to be out of bed." He turned to his mother-in-law. "Would you show Sydney the way?"

Mrs. Caine was friendly, and Sydney relaxed. When she came out of the bathroom, feeling a little more civilized, she returned to the kitchen to discover Maisie and Mrs. Caine seated at the kitchen table, their plates filled.

"Aren't you dining with the family?"

"Don't think we couldn't," Maisie assured her with a grin. "But when Mary Margaret's on her high horse, we're both happier here."

"Could I join the two of you? I'd hate to intrude on the family reunion." She smiled, hoping to charm her way out of the dining room and into the kitchen.

"No, you cannot," a deep voice said behind her. She didn't need to turn around to know Robert had overheard her.

"Robert, I think it would be best—"

He ignored her, taking her arm to lead her through the swinging door. He escorted her across the beautiful room, with an oriental carpet and cherry wood table more elegant than anything Sydney had ever seen.

"Hello, my dear," Robert's mother said, her eyebrows rising. "We thought perhaps you'd gotten lost."

The woman's attitude was beginning to bother Sydney. "Not at all," she said smoothly. "I left a trail of bread crumbs."

There was a stunned silence before several people erupted into chuckles. Sydney didn't bother looking at her hostess. She knew the duchess was not amused.

Penelope, seated to her left, patted her on the shoulder. "That's just like Hansel and Gretel."

"Yes, sweetie, it is," Sydney said with a smile.

And the meal began.

SYDNEY FIGURED she'd ruined any chance of the dowager duchess feeling any kindness toward her. So it surprised her, when she offered to help clear the table after lunch, to find the lady pitching in.

Maisie protested when she and the duchess entered the kitchen with their hands full.

"Here now, I'll clean up."

"We're just helping out," Sydney assured her. "It's small payment for such a lovely meal."

Liz entered the room, carrying several plates. All three older women immediately surrounded her and insisted she sit down. Doing so, she grimaced at Sydney. "They won't let me lift a finger."

"I think you should take advantage of their care," Sydney said with a smile. "I've heard once the baby comes, the mother is kept pretty busy."

"Do you have children yourself?" Lady Hereford asked.

"No, I've never married."

"Perhaps you should change occupations. You might meet more men."

"Actually, I teach elementary school most of the year." Sydney hadn't intended to tell the woman anything about herself, but she was proud of her other job.

"A teacher? That's certainly an honorable profession," the dowager said with a pleased nod. Then, as if she'd momentarily forgotten her place, she looked down her nose. "Not on the same level as being part of the nobility, of course."

"Mary Margaret," Liz protested. "Shame on you. I think teaching is a wonderful profession, though, Sydney, I don't know how you manage an entire classroom of kids like Stacy."

"My grandchild is perfect!" the dowager protested.

Everyone chuckled, and Sydney was surprised to see the lady joining in.

"So why do you drive a truck if you're a school teacher?" Lady Hereford asked, surprising Sydney.

"Because I have financial responsibilities," she said calmly.

"So you thought to become wealthy by entrapping my son?"

Sydney drew a deep breath as the other three women protested. When they quieted, she looked at Lady Hereford. "I have no intention of marrying your son, my lady. Now if you will excuse me, Lady Penelope would like to show me some horses." With a nod to the other ladies, she stood and left the room.

"Mary Margaret, you were very hard on her," Liz protested softly.

"I know. But I had to know."

"Know what?" Maisie asked.

"If she's the one. And she is! Robert will be happy at last."

Mrs. Caine looked confused. "But she said she wouldn't marry him."

"She lied," Lady Hereford said smugly. "After all, who could resist Robert?"

SYDNEY JOINED THE TWO little girls for a trip to the barn. Pete promised Liz to keep an eye on the children, and Robert fell into step with him as he trailed after the trio.

"It's good to see you again," Pete said. "That's the only thing I hate about living here. I seldom see you."

"I know. There's plenty of room at home if you and Liz decide you'd like to move back." Robert would have loved having his brother back but he knew Pete and Liz would never accept his offer.

"Naw, the cattle wouldn't like to travel that far," Pete drawled, grinning at him.

"You're happy?"

"Do you have to ask?" Pete returned. "I have a permanent grin on my face. Even Mother can't find anything that needs fixing. Which leaves her plenty of time to concentrate on you."

Robert groaned. "I've discovered that. She's made my trip a descent into hell. Pen and I were pursued by some very strange women."

"And how does Sydney fit in?"

Robert sent his brother a quick glance, then fixed his gaze on the far mountains. "She gave us a ride."

Pete chuckled. "I thought you seemed a little more interested in her than that."

Robert hoped his cheeks weren't as red as they felt. "She's—uh, she'd make a great mum for Penelope."

"You're not thinking about mothers when you look at her."

Robert had shared many a frank discussion with his little brother as they'd grown up. But perhaps because his words were so accurate, Robert was embarrassed.

"That's not love," he said firmly.

Pete chuckled. "It's part of it. You're also a little protective, though I think she showed at lunch that she can take care of herself."

"She did rather silence Mother, didn't she?"

"Yep."

"Will you help me convince Mother that Sydney's the perfect one for me?"

"You know I'd do whatever I could for you, but Mother's opinion doesn't matter as much as yours. Do you love Sydney?"

"We're compatible. And she'd make a good—"

Pete interrupted. "Come on, Robbie, my boy. Don't give me that mother stuff. That's not enough reason to marry."

"You sound like Sydney," Robert said in irritation, then regretted his words.

"Don't tell me you used the mother line on Sydney?" Pete demanded, his eyebrows raised. "I thought you knew women better than that."

"I won't lie to her," Robert insisted, squaring his jaw.

"Are you sure you'd be lying?"

Robert turned his back and stared into the distance for several minutes. When he again faced his patient brother, he said, "Did you love Liz when you married her?"

"Oh, yeah," Pete drawled. "But I had a hard time admitting it to myself."

"How did you know?"

It was Pete's turn to stay silent. Finally, he said, "I don't think I accepted the fact that I loved her until I lost her. The two weeks it took to run her to earth were the longest I've ever lived. It was facing the rest of my life without her that convinced me I loved her. More than I'd ever loved anyone." He grinned and punched his brother on his arm. "Even you and Mother and Dad."

Life without Sydney. Robert hadn't really faced that possibility. He'd convinced himself that Sydney would accept his proposal. He'd told himself he had too much to offer her. She'd be a fool to refuse wealth, luxury.

Realization struck him. In other words, he'd classified her with all the other women pursuing him. "Damn."

"Looking into the future?" Pete asked softly.

"Yeah. And the immediate past, too. I've gone about everything the wrong way." He couldn't keep his mind off the thought of returning to England without Sydney, the thought of facing the rest of his life without her beside him.

Yet, telling her he loved her—putting himself, his heart, at risk—was frightening.

As if reading his mind, Pete whispered, "It's scary, isn't it?"

"Was it for you?"

"Hell, yes. But not as much as living without her. Besides, we Morrises have never been cowards."

Robert gave a harsh laugh. The generations of family courage didn't seem enough to reveal his need to Sydney. "Maybe you have more of Granddad's cowboy blood than me."

"Nope. You can do it, Robbie. And the reward, if she loves you, is wonderful."

"And if she doesn't?"

"From what I've seen, I'd say that's not likely.

But if she doesn't, at least you'll know you gave it your all.''

Robert nodded his head. But he couldn't help wondering what kind of compensation that was for putting his heart on the line.

HE SPENT THE REST of the day trying to get Sydney alone. But she eluded him, clinging to Penelope, Liz, Maisie, and, once, even his mother.

Much to his surprise, it was his mother who provided the opportunity he needed. As they all sat in the den that evening, she spoke up. "Robert, have you seen the flower garden Mrs. Caine and Liz have put in beside the house? It's quite charming."

"No, I haven't." He looked at Sydney, sitting across the room as far from him as possible. "Come with me to see it, Sydney."

"Oh, no, I—"

"Yes, go with him, child. After all, you won't have time in the morning since you're leaving so early."

Both he and Sydney stared at his mother, surprised at her suggestion. Then Robert leaped to his feet and held out a hand to Sydney.

"Perhaps Mrs. Caine should show us since she and Liz—" Sydney began.

"No!" Robert protested.

"No!" his mother chimed in.

"No, I can't," Mrs. Caine agreed. "I have to finish the blanket I'm making for the baby," she said, as if she'd just pulled the excuse out of thin air.

"Then Penelope—"

"She's playing with Stacy," Lady Hereford assured her. "You two go ahead."

Robert pulled Sydney after him before she could think of anyone else to invite. They stepped out into the velvet softness of an early summer night. The stars shone all over the sky, with no city lights around to interfere.

"It's beautiful here," Sydney said in a hushed voice, but she was tugging on her hand even as she spoke.

"Yes, it is…although our estates in England are just as beautiful. We have several gardens there I'd like to show you." She said nothing, but he noted that stubborn look on her face.

"Can you smell the flowers?" He sniffed the air, hoping to distract her.

She looked at the flowers, and he slipped his arm around her. She jumped back, almost falling over.

"Be careful. You might trip over a rock," he cautioned, drawing her closer to him again.

"Robert, don't—"

"Don't what? Touch you? I can't help it, Sydney. And I don't think you dislike it as much as you want me to believe."

She stiffened. "I never said I disliked touching you, Robert. I said I couldn't marry you. We've already done a lot more than touching."

He swallowed convulsively, remembering just how much touching they'd done. And how much he wanted to do again. "Sydney, you can't leave."

She squared her jaw even more. "I have to, Robert."

"I have something to tell you." He swallowed again. Then, catching her shoulders in his hands, he said, "I love you."

SYDNEY'S HEART almost stopped beating before reality set in. She'd longed to hear those words, but now she knew she'd been dreaming. The dowager duchess had shown her how impossible was any idea she had of marrying Robert.

"Well? Aren't you going to say anything?"

"No, Robert. There's nothing to say."

"But I love you!"

"You perhaps think you do, but I think you're just determined to get your way." As he started to protest, she held up one hand. "Robert, I'm not the right woman for you. If you have any doubts, ask your mother."

"I followed my mother's advice for my first marriage. I was miserable!"

She turned toward the house, determined to end their time together. The sooner she got away from him, the better she would be able to resist the sweetness of his words.

But Robert had no intention of letting her walk away. He pulled her into his arms and let his lips try another brand of persuasion. Sydney, for a brief moment, gave in to his touch. She even wrapped her arms around his neck and pressed against him.

Just for a moment.

Then she pulled away. "I have to go, Robert." She ran for the back door and slipped away while Robert remained standing in the middle of a beautiful garden, stunned by her departure.

He would convince her, he promised himself. If necessary, he would go with her in the morning, leaving Penelope here with his mother.

And he'd stay with her until he convinced her that their union would be the most perfect in the world. Because of love.

Chapter Sixteen

Sydney had been properly raised. She knew what was due her host and hostess: a polite thank-you for letting her stay, and a gracious return invitation, if that were possible. She almost laughed to think of Robert or any of his family dropping by her apartment in New Jersey.

But manners were going to be ignored this time.

She had to get away before she made a huge mistake. Before she let herself believe her dreams could come true. Definitely before she dove back into Robert's embrace and ignored what was best for both him and Penelope.

She paced her room, wondering when it would be best to leave. Finally, she decided she should get a little sleep before she made a long drive alone. Carefully setting the alarm on her wristwatch, she undressed and lay down on the bed.

An hour later, she was still staring at the ceiling. But she was sure that she was doing the right thing—if not for her, at least for Robert and Penelope.

Finally, her body demanded rest, and her eyes drifted closed.

At five o'clock, the buzzer on her watch woke her. It was still dark outside, but she quickly dressed. Then she took the pad and pen she'd found on the dresser and briefly wrote a thank-you to her hosts.

Next, she wrote a sweet note to Penelope, assuring her of her love and asking the child to write her. It would be better to cut off their relationship completely, but Sydney couldn't bring herself to do so.

She wrote nothing to Robert. She wouldn't tell him she loved him. She couldn't promise to see him again.

She couldn't be his duchess.

Gathering her belongings, she slipped out of the room and down the stairs. Even Maisie wasn't up yet. Sydney unlocked the back door, carefully locking it behind her, and headed for her truck.

Once she was behind the wheel, she turned the key and quickly slipped the truck into gear. The motor wasn't quiet, and she didn't want anyone to know she was leaving.

By the time she passed through the gate again, leaving the ranch, her cheeks were wet with tears.

IT WAS STILL DARK outside when Robert woke. He'd set his alarm for six, but it hadn't gone off yet.

Last night, he'd paced the flower garden, trying to make sense of his conversation with Sydney. Trying to figure out how to convince the lady she couldn't leave him. By the time he'd come back into the house, his mother had retired. He had to talk to her. It was time they had a heart-to-heart.

Checking his watch, he decided to get a head start even if it was only five-thirty. His mother would be getting an early start, too, even if she didn't know it yet.

It was almost six by the time he'd showered and shaved and packed a few belongings in a duffel bag. Then he crossed the hall and rapped on his mother's door. Though there was no answer, he opened the door and entered the shadowy interior. Snapping on a lamp, he cheerfully greeted the lump in the center of the big bed. "Good morning, Mother."

A groan was the only response. "Mother, we must speak, and I don't have much time."

She shoved back the cover and raised up on one elbow. "What time is it?"

"Almost six. I'm going to leave with Sydney, and I wanted to be sure you would look after Pen while I'm gone."

"You're leaving? But— With Sydney?"

"Yes, and if you're going to object, save your breath. I've fallen in love with her. She's the only woman who will make me happy." He knew he loved Sydney. He hadn't realized how good it would feel to tell someone, anyone, even his mother.

"Why would I object? I'm the one who said you should remarry. Or have you forgotten?"

"You mean it? You'll accept Sydney as my wife?"

"Of course," the dowager replied, as if there had

been no question. "I was only waiting for you to declare yourself. She'll make a lovely mother for Pen...and any other children you might have."

"But you didn't act as if you approved of her," Robert said, frowning.

"If I had, you would've run the other way. But the girl has backbone, she loves you and Pen, and she's not marrying you for your money. What more could I want?"

Robert leaned forward and kissed her cheek. "I'm glad to hear that, because one of the reasons she turned me down was that she thought you didn't approve of her."

"She turned you down? How dare she?" Lady Hereford screeched even as Robert headed for the door. "Wait, Robert! I have something for you to convince her that I approve."

That halted him in his tracks. "What?"

She struggled from the bed and crossed to the bureau, opening the top drawer. Taking out a small velvet box, she handed it to him. "It's your grandmother's engagement ring, the traditional ring for the future duchess. I think you should start off on the right foot."

He kissed her cheek again. "Thank you, Mother. We'll be back as soon as I convince her."

"Humph! That shouldn't take long, dear boy."

He only hoped she was right.

ROBERT CONSIDERED putting his duffel bag in the truck before he bothered Sydney, but he decided he couldn't wait any longer to see her. So he turned in the other direction and was soon rapping on another door.

Again there was no answer, but he didn't let that stop him. Opening the door, a smile dawning on his lips in anticipation of seeing her, he slipped into the room.

Only to find it empty.

He raced to the window that overlooked the back yard, where she'd parked her truck.

It was gone.

He raced downstairs, through the kitchen where Maisie was already preparing breakfast, to the back porch—as if he might have overlooked the big truck from the second story.

He hadn't. When he erupted into the kitchen again, Maisie stopped him. "She's gone. Left some letters on the table."

"Did you talk to her, see her?"

"Nope. But I heard the truck start up. 'Bout five-thirty, I think. When I got down here, I found the letters."

"There isn't one for me." He noted the letter for Pen and his brother and sister-in-law.

"I reckon she didn't know what to say," Maisie said gently, a lot of sympathy in her eyes.

Robert said nothing in reply. He was already heading for the stairs, prepared to awaken another member of his family.

He was saved the trouble by running into Pete just as he emerged from his bedroom.

"Pete, I need a vehicle. Which one can I take?"

"What for?"

"Sydney left without me. I'm going to catch up with her."

"How long's she been gone?" Pete asked, checking his watch.

"Maisie thinks almost an hour. I need something fast," Robert added, growing impatient.

Pete raised one eyebrow and smiled at his brother. "How about a helicoptor?"

Robert stared, wondering if Pete had lost his mind.

"My neighbor has one he's offered to loan me if we need to get Liz to the hospital in a hurry. I expect he'd be willing to consider this an emergency, too. You'd have to pay him but—"

"Call him!" Robert snapped.

Pete motioned for him to follow, and the two brothers hurried to the kitchen. In no time, Pete arranged for the helicopter to land there in five minutes.

"Thanks, brother," Robert said, accepting a cup of coffee from Maisie.

"No problem. Just don't keep the copter tied up too long. Liz isn't feeling too well this morning." Pete frowned, worry settling down on him.

"If you think you'll need the copter, I'll take a car. It'll just take me a little longer to catch up with her." Robert wasn't going to let Sydney escape, but he didn't want to create any problems for Liz and the baby.

"Naw. Liz would kill me if I did that. We'll be

okay. Here, take this cell phone with you. Let us know when you've got good news.''

Robert accepted the cell phone and drew a deep breath. ''Pete,'' his voice growing solemn, ''you think I'll be able to convince her?''

''I don't have a single doubt, brother. How can she refuse you?''

SYDNEY'S TEARS had stopped. After an hour, all that remained was an occasional sniffle and a dull ache deep in her heart.

She saw her future before her—a future without Robert. Without Pen. ''You should've taken what he offered,'' she muttered to herself. But she knew she couldn't do that. She couldn't stand before God and pretend their marriage was a love match.

Another sob ripped through her. ''Stop it! You made your choice, now live with it.''

She was talking so fiercely to herself that she didn't notice the sound of a helicopter until it was almost above her. It was just coming into her line of vision on the driver's side.

Strange, she'd scarcely seen a vehicle on the road, much less a helicopter. She supposed they had them in Montana, though. Actually, she was approaching the state line of Wyoming, she reminded herself, as if it mattered.

She could barely hear her truck engine now. She leaned forward and looked up, wondering how low the copter was flying.

She almost lost control of the truck as the copter swooped right over her hood.

"Crazy pilot! What's the matter with him?"

She automatically slowed, watching the chopper as it moved forward along the road. Then, to her amazement, it landed in the middle of the highway.

She slammed on her brakes, grateful she had room to stop. When she did, she was going to give that pilot a piece of her mind. He had no business—

Her heart beat double-time as the passenger side of the copter opened, and a tall, handsome man got out.

Robert.

She couldn't breathe. All she could do was stare…and hope.

He bent low and ran from under the rotors, then straightened and headed for her truck. When he reached it, he swung up, opening the passenger door and sitting down in the passenger's seat. He didn't even look at her as he threw his duffel bag down between them.

Fastening his seat belt, he waved to the pilot who lifted off back into the air. Then he said, "Let's go."

Feeling like she was wandering in a maze, Sydney stared at him. "Go where?"

"Wherever you're in such a hurry to go that you couldn't even wait to tell Penelope goodbye." Now he looked at her, accusation in his gaze.

Pain shafted through her. "I left her a note."

"And me? Did you leave me a note?"

At the sound of a car behind her, Sydney moved

her truck, hoping to avoid a collision. Just around the bend was a flat grassy area. She pulled the truck to the side of the road, out of harm's way.

"Robert, I told you I couldn't— No, I didn't leave you a note." When he said nothing, she turned to look at him, something she'd been trying to avoid. "How are you going to get back to the ranch? I can't take you. I don't have time."

"I'm not going back to the ranch until you do have time."

His cool response stunned her. "What do you mean? I have to haul this new load back to Fargo. Then I start my regular route all over again. I'm not coming back to Montana!"

He leaned over and ran a finger down her flushed cheek. "Yes, you are, love. We'll come back to visit often."

"What are you talking—"

This time he stopped her by covering her lips with his.

Sydney couldn't help herself. She reached out for him, so hungry to touch him at least once more. He smelled of open air...and happiness.

She broke away, sobbing. "Don't! Don't do this to me, Robert. You know we can't—"

"Can't what? Be happy? Why not? We deserve it as much as anyone else."

"Robert, you're a duke! I can't marry a duke."

"Why not? Did they pass a law saying dukes must be miserable?"

"No! But I can't make you happy."

"You're doing a great job so far," he assured her, his lips seeking hers again.

"Your mother! We'd both be miserable if your family—your mother thinks I'd make a terrible duchess." She knew he wouldn't have an answer to that. After all, the dowager duchess had made her feelings clear.

"Righto. That's why she sent you this."

Her eyes widened as he pulled out a diamond ring.

"Wh-what is that?"

"You don't recognize diamonds? It's the traditional engagement ring for the future duchess." He tugged on her hand, but she resisted.

"Sydney, she approves of you. I talked to her this morning. She wants very much to welcome you into the family."

"But she was very cool to me."

"I know. Fooled me, too. Pete said Liz knew what she was up to, though. He told me Mother called it reverse psychology. She figured if she welcomed you with open arms, I might back away."

"And would you have?" She had to know.

"No, love. I didn't want to admit that I was in love, but my brother helped me realize I had to take the chance." He framed her face with his hands and his eyes bore into hers with an intense heat. "I love you, Sydney. Pen loves you. Without you, we'll never be happy."

"Oh, Robert, I love both of you, but…"

"From the first moment I saw you you looked better than any duchess I've ever seen. But it's not your beauty that makes you perfect, my love. It's your heart. You have a generous, loving heart. Perfect for me, perfect for Pen. Perfect for any other children we might have.''

''But my mother…''

''Sydney, the least important thing in the world to me is money. Fortunately, I have enough to take care of every relative you have. All I need is you.''

This time when he swept her into his arms, she cooperated with every ounce of her being. When his lips met hers, she thought she'd found heaven. And she never wanted to leave. Except that there was one burning question she had to ask.

''Where did you find a helicopter so quickly?''

''Um, Pete had one on call. Damn, I forgot!'' Robert exclaimed and stopped raining his delightful kisses on her neck.

''What?''

''I was thinking of celebrating our engagement on your bed, but—''

She swallowed, desire rising rapidly. ''Why not?''

''Because Pete called the copter pilot just before we landed to tell him Liz was in labor. I think we should go lend our support for my future heir. At least, future heir until we do get a chance to celebrate. You do want children, don't you, Sydney?''

Tears filled her eyes at the thought. ''Oh, yes. Yes, yes, yes!''

He kissed her again, almost losing control. Finally they separated, smiling at each other. ''Let's head for the hospital, my love,'' Robert ordered.

Sydney began to turn the truck around, then stopped. "But, Robert, I promised Roy I'd be there in the morning."

He brought out the cell phone. "Trade places. I'll drive and you can call Roy. Tell him you're taking up a new profession, that of duchess. There'll be no more truck driving for you, my love."

After she finished talking to Roy, Robert, driving a little above the speed limit, said, "You've got one more call to make."

"To whom?"

"To Pen. Let your new daughter know she's gotten her wish—you as her new mum."

Your daughter.

How she loved the sound of that.

Epilogue

Robert stood with his arm around Sydney, staring into the cradle at the red-faced infant protesting entrance into this new world. "At least, Pete, you know he has healthy lungs."

"Yeah. I think he's even louder than Stacy when she was born."

A nurse arrived with a bottle. "This should soothe the little dear," she said cheerfully, handing the bottle to Liz.

"Want me to feed him, hon?" Pete asked.

Liz smiled, her face showing her weariness. "I think I'd rather you sat here and held my hand. Sydney, would you like to feed James Robert?"

Sydney stared at Liz, wondering if she'd read the hunger Sydney felt when she looked at the tiny baby. "Oh, I'd be honored, Liz. Thank you so much."

Robert beamed at his sister-in-law and followed Sydney to the cradle where the baby kicked and screamed. Sydney gathered up the bundle of life and offered the bottle. James Robert had no intention of making life easy for anyone, and he continued to scream.

Sydney shot a panicked look at Liz.

"He doesn't know much about sucking just yet. Keep offering it. He'll catch on."

Sydney did as she said. Suddenly, the nipple slipped into his mouth and he learned his first lesson.

"He's such a beautiful baby," Sydney whispered.

Robert stared down at the baby and then shared a grin with his brother. Putting his arms around Sydney and the baby, he whispered to her, "Learn all you can, sweet love, because as soon as possible, we're going to have one of our own."

"Well, I hope you're going to marry first, so Mother won't be fussing," Pete said from where he sat beside his wife's bed, his arm around her, his shoulder supporting her head.

Sydney blushed, but Robert only laughed. "Yes, we're going to get married on the ranch—with your permission. Otherwise, I'm promising nothing about the order of events."

"That will make the dowager duchess's day, to say nothing about Pen's," Pete said with a grin. "A grandchild and a new daughter-in-law on the same day."

"Once you two are married, though," Liz began, "we're going to have to find another project for your mother. She won't know what to do without a son to marry off."

"We'll find something for her to do," Robert promised, "because her matchmaking days are over until Pen is ready to marry. And that will be at least thirty years, because I'm not going to let her start dating until then.''

"Maybe we can keep her busy baby-sitting her grandchildren," Sydney suggested softly, her gaze never leaving James Robert's little face.

"Good idea, my love," Robert agreed. "See how well you fit into the family? You understand what's important."

Robert hugged Sydney closer to him, hungering to be alone with her, and yet glad to share the happiness that filled Liz and Pete.

"You'd better get busy making your own heir, 'cause I'm seeing cowboy written all over old Jimbo's face," Pete said, studying his son.

"Pete!" Liz protested. "We're not going to call him Jimbo."

"Well, sweetheart, James seems a bit too proper for this little guy."

Robert grinned. "The American branch of our family is a bit more relaxed than the rest of us."

"I think the American side is bigger, too," Liz said, smiling. "It's four to three right now."

"Another reason to have more babies," Robert said.

Sydney smiled and continued to feed her soon-to-be nephew.

Robert looked to the door. "I hope you're prepared, Liz, because I think the rest of the family has arrived."

Almost before he finished speaking, the door burst

open, admitting Liz's mother, the dowager duchess and two happy little girls.

Stacy ran to her mother and father, but Penelope only had eyes for her father and Sydney, greeting them both with a hug and a loud "Mummy!"

Lady Hereford stood in the center of the room, beaming, offering congratulations all around. Then she claimed the baby from Sydney.

Robert lifted Penelope in his arms and drew Sydney against him. "You don't mind if we marry right away, do you, Pen?"

"No. How about tomorrow? And, Sydney, you can stay at the ranch with us!"

"Yes, sweetie. I get to stay with you wherever you are."

"Except for the honeymoon," Robert added hastily.

"Why?" Penelope asked, a cloud gathering on her face.

"Because honeymoons are only for adults, love. And maybe, then, we'll get to have one of those, too." He motioned to the baby his mother was holding.

"Oh." Penelope considered before saying, "I know all about babies. Do you want me to tell you?"

Sydney and Robert looked at each other, total panic on their faces.

"What I don't understand, though," Pen went on, "is how the stork ties the knot when it doesn't have any fingers."

They smiled at each other and Sydney reached out to hug the child. "Your father will explain later."

Take 2 bestselling love stories FREE

Plus get a FREE surprise gift!

Special Limited-Time Offer

Mail to Harlequin Reader Service®

3010 Walden Avenue
P.O. Box 1867
Buffalo, N.Y. 14240-1867

YES! Please send me 2 free Harlequin American Romance® novels and my free surprise gift. Then send me 4 brand-new novels every month, which I will receive months before they appear in bookstores. Bill me at the low price of $3.34 each plus 25¢ delivery and applicable sales tax, if any.* That's the complete price, and a saving of over 10% off the cover prices—quite a bargain! I understand that accepting the books and gift places me under no obligation ever to buy any books. I can always return a shipment and cancel at any time. Even if I never buy another book from Harlequin, the 2 free books and the surprise gift are mine to keep forever.

154 HEN CH7E

Name	(PLEASE PRINT)	
Address	Apt. No.	
City	State	Zip

This offer is limited to one order per household and not valid to present Harlequin American Romance® subscribers. *Terms and prices are subject to change without notice. Sales tax applicable in N.Y.

UAMER-98   ©1990 Harlequin Enterprises Limited

Presents Extravaganza

25 YEARS!

It's our birthday and we're celebrating....

Twenty-five years of romance fiction
featuring men of the world and captivating women—
Seduction and passion guaranteed!

Not only are we promising you three months of terrific
books, authors and romance, but as an added **bonus**
with the retail purchase of two Presents® titles,
you can receive a special one-of-a-kind keepsake.
It's our gift to you!

Look in the back pages of any Harlequin Presents® title,
from May to July 1998, for more details.

Available wherever Harlequin books are sold.

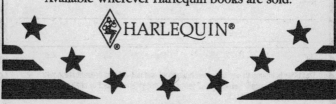

HARLEQUIN®

Heat up your summer this July with

Summer Lovers

This July, bestselling authors Barbara Delinsky,
Elizabeth Lowell and Anne Stuart present three
couples with pasts that threaten their future happiness.
Can they play with fire without being burned?

FIRST, BEST AND ONLY
by Barbara Delinsky

GRANITE MAN
by Elizabeth Lowell

CHAIN OF LOVE
by Anne Stuart

Available wherever Harlequin and Silhouette books
are sold.

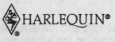HARLEQUIN®

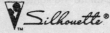Silhouette®

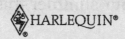

Not The Same Old Story!

Exciting, glamorous romance stories that take readers around the world.

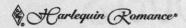
Sparkling, fresh and tender love stories that bring you pure romance.

Bold and adventurous—Temptation is strong women, bad boys, great sex!

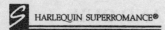
Provocative and realistic stories that celebrate life and love.

Contemporary fairy tales—where anything is possible and where dreams come true.

Heart-stopping, suspenseful adventures that combine the best of romance and mystery.

Humorous and romantic stories that capture the lighter side of love.

MEN *at* WORK

All work and no play?
Not these men!

July 1998
MACKENZIE'S LADY by Dallas Schulze

Undercover agent Mackenzie Donahue's
lazy smile and deep blue eyes were his best
weapons. But after rescuing—and kissing!—
damsel in distress Holly Reynolds, how could
he betray her by spying on her brother?

August 1998
MISS LIZ'S PASSION by Sherryl Woods

Todd Lewis could put up a building with ease,
but quailed at the sight of a classroom! Still,
Liz Gentry, his son's teacher, was no battle-ax,
and soon Todd started planning some
extracurricular activities of his own....

September 1998
A CLASSIC ENCOUNTER
by Emilie Richards

Doctor Chris Matthews was intelligent, sexy
and *very* good with his hands—which made
him all the more dangerous to single mom
Lizette St. Hilaire. So how long could she
resist Chris's special brand of TLC?

Available at your favorite retail outlet!

MEN AT WORK™

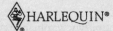 

Look us up on-line at: http://www.romance.net   PMAW2

HARLEQUIN®

A M E R I C A N ◆ R O M A N C E®

COMING NEXT MONTH

#737 DADDY BY DEFAULT by Muriel Jensen
Who's the Daddy?
When Darrick McKeon—the man she never got over—returns with twin babies, demanding if she is the mystery woman who named him as the babies'father and then disappeared, Skye Fennery knows all that stands between her and happiness is a little white lie. So she decides to *make* them a family—if only temporarily.

#738 DREAM BABY by Emily Dalton
Maggie Stern wants nothing to do with her new neighbor, the handsome yet forbidding pediatrician Jared Austin. But then a fan leaves a baby on the doorstep for the infertile character Maggie plays on TV and suddenly she has nowhere else to turn....

#739 A BACHELOR FOR THE BRIDE by Mindy Neff
The Brides of Grazer's Corners
To save her family from disaster Jordan Grazer had to go through with her wedding. But then Tanner Caldwell roared into town and whisked her away for sensuous kisses under the stars. Nothing could make Jordan go back home...except her own promise to say"I do."

#740 TUESDAY'S KNIGHT by Julie Kistler
Kally Malone had always had her life firmly in control. Not anymore! Tim's obsidian eyes and fiery kisses made her all jittery.... And her daughter, Tuesday—seven going on thirty—had a mission: to make Tim part of their family...as the daddy.

AVAILABLE THIS MONTH:

Look us up on-line at: http://www.romance.net